LAW OF THE GUN

He lived by the gun—and expected to die that way, until the kid crossed his trail. Then everything changed. Careful planning had kept Wolf Singleton footloose and away from the law for a long time. It wasn't a bad life—if you knew how to kill. Suddenly there was the kid—eager, full of ideas about becoming a hot-shot outlaw. But the Wolf couldn't let the boy stumble his way into hot lead—not after he found out the kid was his son . . .

LAW OF THE GUN

Paul Evan Lehman

Lansdown
CHIVERS·PRESS·BATH

First published 1958
This Large Print edition published by
Chivers Press
by arrangement with
Donald MacCampbell, Inc.
1992

ISBN 0 7451 5589 8

British Library Cataloguing in Publication Data available

Photoset, printed and bound in Great Britain by
REDWOOD PRESS LIMITED, Melksham, Wiltshire

LAW OF THE GUN

CHAPTER ONE

He sat in a tilted-back chair, heels hooked on the lower rung, the weathered Stetson slanted low on his forehead. His hunched-up position dwarfed the six-foot length of him and the shadow of the hat brim shrouded the upper half of the face with its hawk-keen gray eyes and straight nose. The only features discernible were a clean-shaven, thin-lipped mouth with a square chin beneath it.

It was after sundown, and in the obscurity of the dimly lighted saloon he was as inconspicuous as a lizard on a gray rock. He wanted to be inconspicuous, for one of the few men in the place was Sheriff Ed Grant, who would have given his trigger-finger for a face-to-face meeting.

Grant was standing at the bar sipping warm beer and swapping conversation with the bartender. He had not the slightest idea that the man he had trailed off and on for twenty years was seated only a few yards away. He had noticed the hunched-up figure when he entered the saloon, for he had made it a habit to notice everything within range of his vision; but there had been no tingle of recognition because, for as long as Ed could remember, the man he sought had worn a handsome mustache and the upper lip of this man was bare.

The man was not looking at the sheriff; he was watching a young man who stood at the blackjack table steadily losing his cash. Why he found himself interested in the boy he did not know. He was not one to make friends; he worked alone and lived alone and liked it that way. He had ridden the owlhoot trail for twenty years, holding up stages, banks and even an occasional train, and attributed his life, liberty and pursuit of happiness to the fact that never had there been a partner to betray him; or, either by carelessness or clumsiness, to lead the law to his hide-out. He was a lone wolf, and as though to remind himself that this he must ever be, he had taken the name of Wolf. In the Southwest they had come to refer to him as El Lobo. Not at all original, but expressive enough.

There were less than a dozen men in the saloon, and the blackjack table was the only game running. The young man was its sole customer; he had been playing for nearly an hour and losing consistently. His face was tight and there was a film of sweat on his forehead. It was evident to the hunched-up watcher that he could not afford to lose.

The dealer said, 'You sure are having a run of bad luck, mister.'

The boy nodded jerkily, turned slowly away. He put a hand into the levis pocket and drew out a silver dollar. He held it in his palm and looked down at it, then turned and slapped it on the table.

'Deal.'

He lifted the corners of his two cards, said, 'That's enough.' His eye brightened as he flipped the cards over. A queen and a ten; twenty.

The dealer turned a card. It was an ace. He turned up the second card. It was the jack of clubs; twenty-one. He gave the young man a thin smile and drew the dollar across the table and added it to the pile of coins before him.

The young man pivoted his head and sent a quick glance around the room. Nobody was watching except Wolf, and because of the drawn-down hat the boy was not aware of this. He looked back at the dealer, slid his gun from its holster, held it pressed tightly against his side.

'Stay just like you are,' he whispered, and reached with his left hand for the coins.

'Hey! You can't—!'

The dealer broke it off, but the damage had been done. The sharpness in his voice brought Sheriff Grant's head around. One glance told him the story and he spun on the ball of his foot and drew as he turned.

'Drop it!'

The young man's body jerked as though a bullet had hit it. He hesitated, and Wolf knew he was weighing the chances against him if he were to wheel and fire.

'I said, "Drop it"!'

Reluctantly the young man opened his fingers and the gun dropped on the table. He raised his hands and turned around slowly. Ed Grant had started across the room toward him. Ed was not a big man, but he was strong, rugged, competent and without fear. His face was round and ruddy and his gray hair looked as though he had cut it himself with sheep shears. He was eight years older than Wolf, which put him close to sixty, and he had been sheriff for about half his life.

The young man flashed a desperate, appealing glance about the room, and for a moment his eyes rested on the hunched-up figure on the tilted chair, then hope went out of his face as he resigned himself to arrest.

Wolf unhooked his boot heels, silently lowered the chair legs to the floor, pushed back his hat and stood up. He did this slowly, and Ed Grant, his attention on the young man, was not diverted. Wolf stepped up on the chair, and the gun slid out of its holster and came up to cover the sheriff.

'Stop right there, Ed.'

He said it in a conversational tone, without inflection or emphasis, but Ed stopped dead. Perhaps he knew that voice. For an instant he remained stock still, then very slowly he pivoted his head to look at the man on the chair. Wolf saw his eyes dilate slightly, then narrow.

'Yes, it's me, Ed. I don't have to tell you what to do.'

Ed Grant looked down at his gun, then opened his fingers and let it fall to the floor. Wolf said, 'Kick it under the table,' and he did.

'The rest of you stand hitched,' Wolf said in the same quiet voice. 'Pick up your gun, kid.'

The young man wheeled and snatched up his gun, all ambition and eagerness. He arched the weapon about the room, threatening each occupant in succession.

'I can handle it,' Wolf told him drily. 'Where's your horse?'

'Out front.'

'Get it and take it around back. Mine's there, at the water trough. Fetch him to the back door and be ready for a quick break.'

The young man started for the front door, but Wolf halted him.

'You forgot the money.'

The young man went back to the table, scooped up the coins and put them into his pocket. He strode quickly along the room, passing behind the sheriff so as not to block Wolf's view. Ed Grant still gazed fixedly at the man on the chair.

He said, 'I should have known you, Lobo, even without the mustache. My eyesight must be failing me.'

'We get older every day, Ed.'

The boy was tingling as he pushed through the swinging doors. The sheriff had called this man Lobo. He had heard of El Lobo; everybody had. This was the notorious lone-hand bandit who roamed from Texas to Montana, from Kansas to California, taking what he wanted when he wanted it. And now—El Lobo was helping *him*!

He felt elated, important. El Lobo, the master of them all, had risked capture and perhaps death to help him. Why? He had no time to dwell on it; El Lobo had got him out of this jam and now was dependent on him to win them both free of the saloon and of Sheriff Ed Grant.

He untied his bay horse, mounted it and rode around the saloon to the alley in back. He found the big roan gelding at the watering trough and led it to the rear door of the saloon. He worked it into position with its left flank parallel with the doorway, then drew his gun and whistled shrilly . . .

Inside the saloon, Wolf dominated the room from his chair. 'Don't any of you boys get itchy fingers,' he warned them. 'Barkeep, if there's a scattergun under the counter don't make a grab for it, or you'll come up with a harp.'

'You've crowded your luck too far this time,' said Ed Grant tightly. 'You won't have much of a start and it's still light enough for shooting.'

'You've shot at me for twenty years and haven't hit me yet, but I'll admit I'm a sucker for getting into this. When there was enough money on the tables, I aimed to hold up the joint myself.' His thin lips twisted into a bitter grin. 'So now I'll have to pass it up. I don't know why I horned in unless it was to crow over you, Ed.'

'One of these days,' growled Grant, 'that crow is going to end in a croak.'

From beyond the rear door came a whistle.

Wolf got carefully from the chair, bending a knee, feeling for the floor with the other foot, keeping his hard gaze on them. He moved along against the wall, past the blackjack dealer, then out to the middle of the floor. He backed down the room, felt behind him for the rear door, while they watched him, ready to jump if he made a mistake. He pulled the door open behind him.

The young man said, 'I've got them covered.'

Wolf turned then, saw the boy sitting his horse pointing his Colt at the men inside the room. He wheeled, gripped the horn and stepped quickly into his saddle, keeping low so that the boy could fire over his head, if necessary.

He took the reins the boy handed him, touched the gelding with spurs and sent it leaping along the alley. He kept his crouch, looking back over his horse's rump. The boy had got a slow start but was coming fast now. He sat erect, using his quirt in an effort to get more speed out of his mount. Behind them, a splash of light marked the open doorway, and an instant later he saw the vague forms of men spilling into the alley.

Wolf yelled to the boy, 'Get down! Keep low!'

He saw flashes of gunfire, the reports smothered beneath the pound of hoofs. He saw the boy bend over the pommel, and turned his head to concentrate on riding.

He led the way southward at a dead gallop until it was completely dark, then veered sharply to the west. The boy kept the same distance behind him. After another half hour, Wolf pulled up and the other horse broke stride, came up at a trot and halted beside him. Wolf was listening for sounds of pursuit and now he heard the faint drum of hoofs far to the southeast.

He said, 'You can sit up now. We've got to make time. There's a big stretch of desert to the west and we've got to cross it tonight.'

There was no light now but that of the stars, and by it he saw the boy push himself slowly erect. Wolf's lips curved in scorn. Scared; scared stiff. Well, he'd pilot the kid across the desert and then turn him loose.

They set out westward again, holding down

to a running walk, knowing that Ed Grant would halt his party to listen for hoofbeats just as they had. After ten minutes or so, Wolf saw the young man sag over the horn again and knew that it was something other than fear which caused it. He reached out, seized the reins, and pulled both horses to a halt.

The young man sat up. 'What's—matter?'

Wolf swore. 'You were hit back there!'

'Not bad. Keep—going.'

Wolf spurred closer, did some exploring with fingers. The coat was soggy with blood and there was a tear in the cloth just below the left shoulder blade. Underneath the coat the shirt was saturated, and blood was running down into the boy's levis. The bullet, as nearly as Wolf could tell, had passed between two ribs, gouging out quite a chunk of flesh.

He swore again. This was a complication he had not foreseen. A slug, fired at random by Grant or one of them from the rear of the saloon, had struck the boy after most of its force had been spent by distance. Luck; just plain luck.

'I tell you, I'm all right,' the boy protested.

'You'd better be. We got to cross the desert tonight.'

The faint thud of hoofs was in the east now. Sheriff Ed Grant had changed course also.

'He knows that desert is the only place we can lose him,' said Wolf grimly. 'You sure you can stick it out?'

'Sure, I can.'

They set out again, the wounded man trying to hold himself erect. They were moving much too slowly; they must make time if they were to cross the desert tonight. The boy clung tightly to the horn, pushing himself erect again when his body momentarily sagged. They had covered about a mile when he slid abruptly sideways out of the saddle. He clung to the reins and dragged the horse to a stop.

Wolf rode back to where he lay and sat for some seconds looking down at him. The thing to do, he told himself, was to get out of there and leave the boy where he was. Ed Grant would find him and take care of him; the kid would do a few months in the calaboose and then be free again. And, unencumbered, Wolf could make it across the desert without trouble.

Perhaps it was reluctance to concede even such a small victory to Ed Grant which drove Wolf to do what he did. He got down, lifted the unconscious young man and tied him securely in the saddle with his lariat.

He started again, heading westward, leading the other horse. He tried to force the pace but the lead horse kept lagging. When he halted briefly to listen, he could still hear the posse behind him. Ed Grant must have guessed that he'd try to make the desert crossing.

Wolf pulled the other horse up beside him,

took a look at the boy. He lay in his bonds like a bundle of clothes. He was unconscious, and Wolf knew that if the bleeding was not stopped soon he would die.

Again Wolf debated leaving him, but stubbornness goaded him. He'd beat Ed Grant yet. He turned southward, letting the horses walk. When next he stopped to listen, he could hear the posse distinctly, but they seemed to be holding a westward course.

He had to do something about the boy real quick. There was no water that Wolf knew of for miles, but two filled canteens hung on his saddle and there was grub in his bags.

He kept pushing southward, and presently the moon lifted itself into view. It was two in the morning when he started to climb a range of barren, rugged hills. He knew the region fairly well, knew of a hide-out of sorts. None too good, but it must do.

He came to the place at last, a rock-studded ravine which had been blocked at one end by an old rock fall. In some manner the bottom boulders had interlocked so as to form a shallow cavern some twenty feet square and ten feet high. There was no shrubbery to conceal the entrance and no way out except the way one came in. There was room for both men and their horses, but if the sheriff found them there it would be surrender or die. And Wolf had nothing to gain by surrendering.

The hairs on the back of his neck prickled and a chill ran along his spine as he entered the cave. He felt the cold fear of the wild beast that sensed a trap that desperation forced it to enter.

In the east, dawn was painting the sky gray . . .

CHAPTER TWO

He got the boy off his horse, then put both animals in the rear of the rock chamber. He took a candle from his saddlebag and lighted it and examined the boy's wound.

Dried blood had cemented the boy's undershirt to the bullet hole. He cut away shirt and undergarment, then soaked the cloth which still adhered to the flesh until he could remove it. The wound was not a serious one; the boy had fainted from loss of blood.

Wolf sat on his heels and scowled resentfully at the unconscious young man, cursing himself for a fool to interfere in the first place, and for a double-damned fool for not leaving the boy back there on the flat. Now, as a result of his foolishness, he was trapped in this impossible cavern, and might lose his life because of it.

He had stripped the boy to the waist. A well-built lad he was, almost as tall as Wolf, with wide shoulders, deep chest and narrow waist. In the relaxation of unconsciousness, his features were almost childlike, although there was strength in the square chin. Wolf guessed his age at not more than nineteen. Around his neck was a cord, and depending from it was a tarnished gold locket. The locket would contain a picture; probably, thought Wolf, that of the boy's sweetheart.

He made an impatient gesture and stood up. He went to the boy's horse and unstrapped his blanket roll. He opened it and took a clean undershirt from it. With this he made a compress to cover the wound and a band with which to hold it in place. He spread the boy's blanket, moved him onto it and covered him.

The boy would need food and plenty of it, and all Wolf had was the small stock he carried in his saddlebags. If they were pinned down here for any length of time they would need water, not only for themselves but also for the horses. The nearest spring he knew of was ten miles away.

He went outside the cavern and stood listening. He could not see the eastern horizon but the stars above the ravine were dimming and daylight would soon come. He climbed the bank of the ravine and found himself on a rocky plain. There was greasewood here and a little mesquite. He gathered what he could, being careful not to break branches where they would be seen. Ed Grant was an old hand and could read sign like an Indian.

He made three trips from and to the cave carrying brush; then, before it was light enough for the thin haze of smoke to be seen, he built a small fire and stewed some dried venison, boiling it in a large tin cup until all the strength had been extracted. He set the broth aside to cool and made a pot of coffee, then let the fire die and extinguished the candle as daylight crept into the ravine and through the entrance to the cave.

The boy opened his eyes. He looked up at the man who crouched beside him, then turned to take in the lighted oblong of the rocky entrance. 'Where are we?' The voice was weak.

Wolf told him succinctly, his irritation at the boy, as the instrument of his own foolishly impulsive act, returning.

'We got nothing to be happy about. We're about as safe here as we would be out on the flat behind a rock.' He picked up the tin cup and abruptly thrust it at the boy. 'Here. Drink this. We can't move until you get back some of your strength.'

The boy took the cup, his gaze at Wolf. 'Why did you do it? I mean, stick with me like this.'

'I don't know. If I had it to do again, I wouldn't. Now drink that.'

The boy drank the stew, handed back the cup. 'You should have left me, Lobo. Back there when—'

'Where'd you get hold of that name?'

'I heard the sheriff call you that. I've heard of you—plenty. You are El Lobo, ain't you?'

'The name's Wolf.'

'Sure. In Spanish, it's Lobo.' He relaxed on the blanket. 'But I can't figure why you risked your neck for me.'

'That makes two of us,' said Wolf shortly.

He went to his horse and got a can of condensed milk from his pack. He punched two holes in the lid, poured some of the thick fluid into the cup and diluted it with water. He shoved it at the boy.

'Drink it.'

While the boy drank, Wolf got a flannel shirt from the boy's belongings. 'I'll help you into this. Had to use the undershirt. Bandage.'

The boy sat up and Wolf worked his arms into the sleeves and helped tuck the garment into his pants. 'Lie down and get some sleep.'

The boy sank back on the blanket, but he did not close his eyes. 'You haven't asked me anything about myself.'

'Why should I?'

'I don't know. You got the right. My name's Dave; David—'

'Shut up, Dave. Go to sleep.'

He went to the cave entrance to look and listen. Young Dave noticed how he walked, quietly, effortlessly, like the animal whose name he bore. Wolf was past middle age, but he was still as supple as a willow bough and as tough as hickory.

Dave's eyes were warm. This man, the notorious El Lobo, was risking his life to take care of him. A deep gratitude was mixed with his wonder. Some day, perhaps, he could repay El Lobo.

Wolf looked southward along the bed of the ravine. Stones, sand and gravel; not a sprig of vegetation. Dry, dreary, desolate. The banks rose to a height of fifty feet, and a man or horse had to take a diagonal course in ascending or coming down.

He moved up the ravine for a hundred yards or so, then turned to look back. He could make out the figure of the boy lying on his blanket; the horses were hidden in the gloom at the rear of the cave.

Wolf shook his head. The sun was in the east and not very high, but for a couple hours before and after noon it would turn its searchlight along the ravine and light up every corner of their hiding place.

He walked back to the cave. There was nothing he could do about it but hope that Ed Grant and his posse would not enter the ravine during that period. He munched dry food from his pack and washed the stuff down with a can of tomatoes. Dave was sleeping and must be fed again when he awoke.

He went outside again, stood listening for

some seconds, then climbed the west bank of the ravine. At the top he lay flat and looked across the sandy stretch. The low hills which they had traversed were like the waves of a motionless, dun-colored ocean. There was no creature, still or moving, within his vision.

He returned to the cave, selected only the driest of his wood, and kindled a small fire and made another stew in the coffeepot. He poured it into the tin cup and the empty tomato can, then made a fresh batch of coffee.

Dave awakened and Wolf made him swallow as much of the stew as he could hold. Then he opened a can of peaches, poured half the contents into the tin cup and added condensed milk and water.

'Eat it. You need blood. We can't stay here much longer.'

Dave was sitting up, but his hands trembled with weakness when he ate. He ate the peaches, then tried to roll a cigarette. He was unable to do it and Wolf did it for him. The horses were stamping and whinnying softly.

Dave said, 'They're hungry. Nothing for them, is there?'

'They need water most.'

'We'll get out of here tonight, Wolf. I can make it. I feel great.'

'We're leaving, no matter how you feel. Ed Grant will find this ravine almost any time now. Stand up.'

Dave got to his knees, raised slowly to his feet while Wolf looked on critically. Dave swayed, almost fell.

'Lie down.'

'But I can do it—give me a chance! Soon as I start moving about—'

'Lie down before you fall down.'

Reluctantly, Dave lowered himself to the blanket. 'Look, Wolf. I'll be all right by tonight. If I'm not, you can tie me on my horse.'

'Don't worry; I will. We've got to get out of here. The horses are getting restless and they'll make enough noise to give us away if Grant gets close enough to hear them.'

'How much water we got?'

'I have one full canteen; yours is about half full. We'll head for the spring this side of the desert. It's tonight or never.'

Light crept into the cave as the sun moved to the south. They crowded back as far as they could, but the light searched them out and they felt naked and exposed. Wolf walked up the ravine and when he turned he could see the boy and both horses. A man coming along that ravine could not miss seeing them.

Once more he climbed the bank and made his way across the flat to the ridge. He looked out over the terrain and then movement to the southwest caught his attention. A small body of horsemen rode slowly along the crest of a hogback not more than two miles away. He counted six of them. They were traveling from south to north, and presently they rode into a defile and he lost sight of them. He watched for nearly an hour but did not sight them again.

Wolf's face tightened; he had to make his decision right now. If they waited until dark it might be too late; if they started while it was still light, the boy, in his weakened condition, would be too much of a handicap. They would be captured or killed. It took but a moment for him to make up his mind.

He returned to the cave to find Dave asleep. He stood for a moment looking down at him. The boy must be left behind; El Lobo had too many chips in the pot to risk sticking with him any longer. The posse were searching somewhere to the west; if he left at once he could ride eastward and then circle them. He would leave the remaining grub and water for Dave, and if the posse by some chance failed to find him, he could leave under his own power the following night.

Dave opened his eyes, blinked up at him, then pushed himself up on an elbow.

'What is it? What's wrong?'

'I saw the posse a couple miles to the southwest. They're not overlooking anything and they won't miss this ravine. The two of us can't make it in daylight, not with you in this shape.'

Dave considered him gravely and Wolf experienced a feeling of frustration. How could he tell the kid that he was deserting him to save his own skin?

The boy solved the problem for him. 'Look, Wolf: You say they're searching off to the west. Take your horse and get out of this ravine and head east. Right now. When you've got a good start, I'll build a fire outside the cave. They'll see the smoke and head straight for here. You can circle around them and head for the desert. I'll tell them you left me last night and I don't know where you are. It's the only thing to do.'

'That's just what I aimed to do.'

'Good! You get out of here fast. You're El Lobo; they'll hang you if they catch you. I'm only David Singleton and the only time I broke the law was when I held up that tinhorn gambler. Here!' He put his hand into a pocket and took out the money he had taken from the blackjack dealer. He thrust it at Wolf. 'Take this. Maybe you'll need it.'

Wolf stared at him. 'Singleton? Where you from?'

'Wyoming, near Sheridan. Here; take this money.'

'How long have you lived there?'

'I was born there. My grandfather has a ranch there.'

'Your father and mother living?'

Dave shook his head. 'Mother died last

spring. Father was killed in the war before I was born. That's why Ma left Kansas and went back to her folks.'

Wolf was leaning forward, every muscle taut. He spoke with an effort. 'Was your father's name—William?'

'No; George. Why?'

Wolf sucked in his breath, expelled it. Then aware of his tenseness, he relaxed and slowly straightened.

'I knew a William Singleton who died years ago. Thought for a minute you might be kin to him. Any William Singleton in the family?'

'No. My father had no brothers or sisters. Now you take this jingling money and get gone!'

'Put it away!' Wolf took off his hat and wiped his forehead with his scarf. 'I've changed my mind. That posse has a lot of ground to cover and they'll camp when it gets dark. We'll start out then, ride east and circle.'

'Don't stay on my account,' said Dave heatedly. 'You've done enough for me already.'

'Did I tell you I was doing it on your account? I got my own reasons for what I'm doing. Now put away that change and lie back, like I tell you!'

Dave returned the money to his pocket. 'I won't forget this, Wolf. Never. I learn quick and won't make any more fool kid plays. I'd like it a lot if you'd let me ride with you.'

'Not a chance, kid. I've always ridden alone and I always will. If we get out of this, you're going back to Wyoming and marry that girl of yours and settle down to raising cows and kids.'

The boy looked puzzled. 'What girl?'

'The one whose picture you're carrying in that locket.'

'Pretty, ain't she?'

'I didn't look at it.'

'Well, she is. But she ain't my sweetheart; she's my mother.' He drew out the locket, opened it with a thumb nail. He slipped the cord over his head, held the locket out to Wolf. 'She's beautiful. Look at her.'

Wolf took the locket. For a long moment he stared at the picture, then he snapped the locket shut, handed it back to Dave. He said gruffly, 'Grab that cup and down more of that stew. If you're not in shape to travel tonight, I'll leave you flat.'

He went out into the ravine. He no longer walked like the animal whose name he had taken; he stumbled several times and it took real effort to get to the top. There he slumped down on a rock and took off his hat and again mopped his forehead. His face was haggard, his eyes tortured.

There could be no mistake. The picture had clinched it. He knew now why the boy had stirred such a deep interest in him, why he had risked his life to protect David Singleton.

The man who called himself Wolf had been christened George Singleton. This boy was his son.

CHAPTER THREE

He sat there for a long time, his thoughts going back, twenty years. Yet just under the surface, his mind was fully alert to his present danger; it was like sleeping always with one eye open . . .

He had been married a year, had filed on a homestead under the recent law, and had a few head of cattle which he hoped in time to build into a large herd. He had little interest in the war between the North and the South. Then he had met William Clarke Quantrill, teacher, gambler, horse thief, and now Confederate soldier.

Quantrill was organizing a band of cavalry, reckless adventurers like himself, for the purpose of raiding Yankee communities in Kansas and Missouri.

'Ride with me,' Quantrill had argued, 'and you can build up your herd at the expense of Yankee ranchers. Burn them out, take their stock, add them to your own.'

War seemed to make theft legitimate. George Singleton left his young wife with the excuse that duty called him, loyalty to the Southland where he had been born.

History tells the sordid story of Quantrill and his guerrilla band. It is a story of robbery, pillage, rapine and murder under the guise of war. George Singleton became callous and hardened; the death of a human being came to mean nothing to him. When Quantrill was killed and the band broken up, Singleton returned to his wife and his homestead.

He had added no stock to his herd, and he had saved little of the loot which had been his share, and when it was gone he could conceive of but one way of securing what he needed. Singlehanded he had held up a small bank and in the getaway had killed the town marshal. He had to leave Kansas, and quick.

His years with Quantrill had fitted him for the life of an outlaw, a hunted fugitive. In Colorado he ran out of cash and held up a gambling dive. He did it alone and got away with several thousand dollars. But again he had to kill. From that time on it had been one armed robbery after another, but he made it a practice never to pull two successive holdups in any one state. He roamed the country, but he did not milk the cow dry. Sometimes a period of six months passed between robberies. He wore a mask whenever it was practicable and changed horses and outfits frequently.

He thought often of the young wife he had deserted, but dared not risk visiting or communicating with her, remembering the long list of wanted men who had had their careers and their lives abruptly terminated through the agency of some loved one. When, years later, he had returned to the homestead he had found it deserted, his wife gone...

Wolf pounded his knee with a fist and groaned, 'Why didn't she tell me? Why didn't she?'

It would have been so different had he known a son was on the way. There would have been no robberies, no killings, no tenacious Ed Grant. But perhaps Mary herself had not known. The child had been born after her return to her parents' home in Wyoming.

Now here he was, holed up in a miserable cave that might become a death trap with a son who believed his father had died an honorable death in the war. They had told him that, of course, so that he would never know the kind of man his father really was, a renegade, a thief and a killer. He was thankful now that, in order to shield Mary, he had taken the name Wolf; he was thankful, too, that Ed Grant, the only one who knew his real identity, had aided in the deception by keeping the name George Singleton off the record. He had known Ed in the old days, and Ed had known Mary.

Thought of Ed Grant shook him out of his bitter memories. He got up effortlessly, already aware that his danger had now increased. Now, he realized grimly, he had much more to fight for than just himself. He must get David—his son—to a safe place.

He started across the flat, and now his stride was once more that of the wolf. He thought swiftly as he walked. After he got David away from Ed Grant, then what? He knew that to the boy he was a hero, a romantic Robin Hood; the boy was eager to follow the owlhoot trail under the sponsorship of the man known as El Lobo. The seed of outlawry had been planted when he attempted to hold up the blackjack dealer, and had taken root when he learned that the man who had made his escape possible was the famous El Lobo. If Wolf refused to take the boy with him, then certainly David would turn outlaw on his own. He'd seen it happen often enough.

Wolf swore harshly. David was his son; he was responsible for keeping the youngster from making an irrevocable mess of his life and what could be—yes, *must* be!—a fine and decent future. But how could he get the boy on the right path and keep him there? To tell David of their relationship was unthinkable; it would only strengthen his desire to share his father's life. Yet there must be a way, and he must find it.

The sun was low now and its rays would no longer flood the cave. With the coming of dusk the posse would make camp, probably in some hollow where their fire would not be seen.

He returned to the cave and found David on his feet, keeping the restless horses in the rear of the cave.

'They came near to bolting,' he told Wolf. 'They need water. Can't we spare them a swallow?'

'We'll give them a little tonight before we pull out. You finish that stew?'

'Yes.'

'There's half a can of peaches and some condensed milk left. I'll fix it for you.'

'You got anything to eat?'

'There's some grub in my pack. Sit down and save your strength; you'll need it tonight.'

He shooed the horses back into a corner, anchored them there by putting heavy stones on the hanging reins. He poured condensed milk over the peaches, added a little water, and gave the can to David. He gnawed on venison and hard bread. He did not touch the precious water.

When they had finished, the sun was completely gone and the cave was a black maw.

Wolf said, 'Be dark enough to leave in half an hour. Think I'd better tie you on your horse?'

'No. I'm all right now.'

'You're weaker than you think, son.'

The word rolled off his tongue like music. Son! His son! His and Mary's. He knew his expression had softened, but it was too gloomy in the cave for the boy to see.

Dave said, 'Coming from you, I like that. It's what Ma used to call me—son.'

Dave finished the peaches, declared he felt great, and they packed their gear and strapped their rolls on the horses. Wolf tightened the cinches.

'Let's take a look at that side of yours before we pull out,' Wolf said.

Dave seated himself on a stone and Wolf helped him remove his shirt. He lighted the candle, removed the bandage. The wound was raw, but there had been no bleeding and it did not appear to be infected. Wolf refolded the compress, put ointment on it, bound it in place. He helped Dave on with his shirt.

'We'll start now, but we'll give the horses some water first.'

He took the full canteen from his saddle, removed his hat and told the boy to hold it. He poured half the water into the hat and Dave let his horse drink. The animal sucked up the water, nuzzled the hat for more.

Wolf poured the remaining water into the hat and the second horse was given its share. For themselves they had the water in the boy's half-filled canteen. If the spring on the edge of the desert had dried up, this would have to last until they had crossed.

Wolf helped Dave into the saddle, handed him the reins. 'I'll walk until we reach the top.

We'll have to tackle the bank on a slant. Follow me close.'

He extinguished the candle, put it into his pocket and led his horse to the cave entrance. There he stopped out of force of habit to listen.

They both heard it, the metallic ring of iron shoes on stones. The sound blended with others, the jingle of bit chains and the voices of men speaking indistinguishable words. The gloom in the ravine was too deep for visibility, but they did not need to see to know that this was Ed Grant and his posse.

'Make a break for it?' the youngster whispered.

Wolf glanced quickly up the side of the ravine. Against the lingering daylight which outlined the brink, they'd be skylined like clay pigeons in a shooting gallery.

'Not a chance,' he whispered back. 'Pull back a little and stay there. If they come too close, I'll start firing. When I do, you head for the west bank and go up.'

'But—!'

'Damn it, I'm giving the orders; you do what I say.'

'Sure, Wolf.'

Dave backed his horse farther into the cave, and Wolf stood waiting, watching the dark mass which materialized in the ravine ahead of him. It was possible that Ed Grant knew of this cave and planned to camp in it. If so, he would fire and immediately break for the east bank, hoping to draw their attention away from Dave. He put a foot in the stirrup, grasped the horn, stood poised.

The dark mass halted and Ed Grant's voice said, 'We'll camp here. The ravine is plugged up ahead and that will make it easy to hold the horses.'

'You sure it's plugged, Ed?' asked another voice.

'Take a look at the skyline. Both banks caved in. Yes, it's plugged, all right. Tom, climb up and look around for wood. Ought to be some mesquite and greasewood up there.'

Leather creaked as men lifted themselves out of saddles. Then came sounds which told Wolf that the horses were being stripped of their gear. Bits of talk came to them:

'I been settin' straight up and down so long I'm stiff as a fence post. Sure will feel good to stretch out.'

'How long you aim to keep us at it, Ed?'

'We'll finish these hills tomorrow by noon. If they ain't here, there's no other place to look.'

'I'll give anybody eight to five that they made it across the desert. That El Lobo knows his way around.'

The horses were hazed closer to the cave and presently a little flicker of flame appeared beyond them and grew until Wolf could see their shapes between him and the fire. He turned his horse carefully and led him back to where Dave waited.

Dave said out of the darkness, 'What do we do?'

'We wait.'

'But we can't stay here! Come daylight, they'll spot us sure.'

'I know. Hold my reins and stay put.'

He went back to the cave entrance. The fire was blazing now and he could see the silhouettes of men as they moved about preparing supper. Two figures came along the bed of the ravine, and Wolf, invisible to them because of the blackness behind him, drew his gun. The two halted a dozen yards away.

One of them said, 'It's a good thing we watered the horses back there at that creek. Should have let them fill up with grass, too, but you were in such a hell of a hurry.'

'I wanted to search as much of this country as we could before dark,' said Ed Grant. 'I'm sure I winged the young one; seen him flop over in the saddle. If I hit him hard enough they might have to hole up somewheres, but with a whole day to rest he might be in shape to travel tonight. Even a wounded man can travel pretty far on a horse in ten, twelve hours.'

From the direction of the fire came a shout, 'Come and get it!' and Ed and his companion walked back toward the camp.

It was dark on the brink of the ravine now

and although there was yet no moon, the stars were bright. Wolf slipped his gun into its holster and started back. He heard one of the horses in the cave nicker softly and it alarmed him until he remembered that anybody in the posse would think the sound had come from their own horses.

He whispered, 'Son, we've got to make our move now, while they're eating. Give me my reins.'

He got into his saddle and led the way to the mouth of the cave. 'I'm going to stampede the horses up the ravine,' he said quietly. 'They're spooky and it won't take much to get them going. As soon as I start shooting, I want you to head for the west side and climb the bank. Take it at a slant. Ride straight north by the North Star, at a slow lope; I'll go up the east bank, circle north and join you. Got it?'

'Sure, Wolf. I got it.'

Wolf rode out into the ravine, drew his Colt. He spurred the horse into a run, giving vent to the weird coyote cry, keeping it up, and firing his Colt into the air. Against the blaze of the campfire he saw the horses wheel, start running; he saw the men around the fire come to their feet. He fired three more shots, and the horses broke into a frantic gallop. As they pounded past the fire, men jumped out of their way.

He wheeled the roan gelding and sent it

lunging up the east bank on a diagonal course. He glanced to the west; Dave should be on his way up but the bank was so dark that he could not see him, nor could he hear his horse above the sounds of shouting men and the stampeded horses.

He fired the last shell in his gun, hoping to hold the attention of the posse, and knew he had succeeded when he heard answering shots and the scream of lead. They kept firing in his general direction, and he wheeled his horse and sent him up on the opposite tack. He reached the top, crouched low as he went over the rim. He was headed south and kept going in that direction for a hundred yards, then cut to the east and across the rock flat.

Up here there was some light from the stars, and by it he saw two men scramble over the lip of the ravine. There was a stab of flame and a bullet sped by him and he knew the weapon from which it had come was a rifle. He had to get out of range quickly, and he did it by keeping dead eastward and crouched low. Both men were on foot and could not follow.

How much of a start had he? It depended on how far the posse's horses would run. There should be enough of a lead, but with a wounded kid to look after, every yard and every second counted.

He cut northward, riding hard, and presently began bearing to the west. At the end of half an hour he sighted Dave ahead of him and slightly to his left. Dave saw him and came riding to meet him. Wolf halted to listen, heard no pound of hoofs.

'You did it!' said the boy warmly. 'Wolf, that sure was something to see!'

'We're not out of it by a long shot. How are you?'

'Fine! You're a tophand medico!'

They rode steadily for two hours, stopping occasionally to listen and to breathe the horses. Wolf, watching Dave anxiously, saw him clinging to the horn. They came to the spring, and when they found it flowing it took a load from Wolf's mind. The horses had sweated out just about all the moisture in them, and the arid desert crossing was ahead. He had to lift Dave out of the saddle.

The horses trailed their reins to the spring and drank avidly. He put Dave on the ground and dragged them away from the water. He held the reins while they cropped at the grass, and when they had eaten for a longer time than he liked, he gave them some more water. Dave was on his feet again, insisting that he could ride. Wolf said, '*S-s-s-h!*' and stiffened, listening. The distant beat of shod hoofs against the rock flat reached them faintly.

'He's guessed we're headed for the desert,' Wolf said grimly. 'We've got to make time before the moon comes up. I'm going to tie you aboard, because this time there'll be no stopping.'

Dave submitted to being tied on his horse, Wolf binding both feet in the stirrups and then tying the stirrups together with a rope passed under the horse's belly. Dave could sag, but he couldn't fall.

They headed out into the desert, and as the sand grew deeper the horses' pace slowed to a walk. Now, with the sand deadening the noise of their progress, they could hear the sound of hoofbeats on the rocky shelf behind them. The starlight was bright and on that vast level expanse they felt as though they were riding under floodlights. At the end of half an hour, they could no longer hear the posse and knew Ed and his men had ridden out into the desert sand.

Wolf began bearing more to the south. 'Here's hoping,' he said, 'that Ed keeps straight west.'

The pace was easier on Dave and he kept erect by holding to the saddle horn. Both of them scanned the desert behind them until their necks ached from turning. Suddenly Wolf swore and pulled up short. He dropped from his horse and thrust the rein at Dave.

'I sighted them! Hold my reins until I cut you loose.'

He slashed the ropes which bound Dave, took both sets of reins as the boy got off his horse. He dragged both horses to the ground and they sat on the animals' heads to hold them down, crouching as low as they could.

The horsemen appeared as a dark mass against the starlight, not half a mile behind them and to the south. They waited with drawn guns, holding their breaths, two small mounds on a sea of sand, hoping to be mistaken for clumps of desert growth.

The mass moved slowly, a dark cloud against the starlit sky. But the posse approached no closer, and it seemed hours before they were lost in the gloom off to the west.

Wolf got up and his horse scrambled to its feet. He had to help Dave to get on his mount, but this time he did not tie him. Ed Grant would continue on his course to the far side of the desert in the hope that his quarry had not turned off.

Toward midnight a strong breeze came up which would erase any vestige of their tracks in the dry sand, and for the first time in many years, Wolf found himself humming tunelessly. He felt lighthearted, almost happy. Not because he had escaped—he knew he could not hope to escape forever—but because he had found his son, and Dave was free.

CHAPTER FOUR

Daylight found them at the edge of the desert, and Wolf selected a place where the ground beyond the sand was stony and hard. When they had gone a short distance, he got off his horse and backtracked, carefully erasing what small sign they had made. Dave, white of face and tight of lip, clung grimly to his saddle horn.

At the foot of a gentle slope which led upward into a range of naked hills a fresh spring bubbled up among some rocks and tules. The horses nickered thirstily, but Wolf held them to their course.

'Ground's damp there,' he explained. 'We'd leave tracks. Water on the other side.'

They climbed steadily, winding around huge boulders, descending shale slides, following ravine beds and traversing dry washes and gullies. They crossed a rocky plateau, and at noon reached the spring Wolf had mentioned. After refreshing themselves and their horses, they resumed their way toward another low range of hills nearby. Wolf indicated them with a nod.

'On the other side is what I call home. We'll make it in a couple of hours or so.'

There were trees on this second range, scattered and scrawny, but a relief from the stark slopes over which they had passed. At the crest they saw below and ahead of them a grassy basin in which cattle grazed. On its far side, at the foot of still another wooded range, were ranch buildings, matchboxes at that distance; and some five miles southwest of these was another, larger cluster of dwellings which Dave knew must be a town of sorts.

Wolf bobbed his head toward the latter. 'Santa Anita, a Mexican town, but there's a store there, and a cantina. The ranch is mine.'

Dave looked a question.

'Oh, I don't run it; I hired the man I bought it from to do that. I told him I'm a cattle buyer, that's why I'm away so much. The deed is made out to Christopher Jones. Nobody around here knows who I really am.'

They started the descent to the basin, and after a short while Wolf chuckled. 'A mustache makes a big difference in a man's appearance, especially one like I had before I shaved it off, a few months back. That was the handsomest clump of foliage you ever saw. All the descriptions of me bore down real heavy on that mustache. It got to be the first thing men looked for—sort of a personal trade-mark.'

When they reached the basin, Wolf did not head for the buildings on the other side, but turned eastward to follow the base of the hill. They rounded a knoll and came to a cabin built of logs and adobe. There was a pole corral at the edge of the trees behind the cabin, and running through the corral was the overflow of a spring. At one side was a shed, open in the front, and in it was a buckboard.

'Used to be a line camp,' explained Wolf as he lifted himself from his saddle. 'I live here.'

He untied Dave and helped him to dismount. The boy wobbled on his feet and Wolf put his arm around him, being careful about the wound, and helped him into the cabin. He made him lie down on a bunk and started a fire in the stove.

'We'll have some real grub now.'

He went outside and off-saddled and staked out the horses. When he returned the fire was going and he put water on to boil. He worked Dave out of his shirt and sterilized and redressed the wound.

'Looks pretty good, considering,' he announced. He covered Dave with a blanket and told him to sleep.

He took his rifle and went outside, and presently a shot awakened the dozing Dave. He was half asleep when Wolf came in carrying a wild turkey. He tiptoed to the stove, got the pot of boiling water and sneaked out again. When he came in again he carried the dressed turkey, but Dave did not hear him because he was sleeping soundly.

Wolf stopped beside the bunk and stood for some minutes looking down at his son. Again the wonder of it struck him, and an odd wave of tenderness swept over him. Again he searched his mind for a way to kill Dave's desire to emulate the famous El Lobo. The boy had taken the first downward step when he held up the gambler; the inclination to keep on was there, strengthened by his association with the fabled outlaw who had thumbed his nose at sheriffs for twenty years, and whose name was legendary throughout the western frontier.

Wolf doubted that he could talk Dave out of it. A lecture by El Lobo on the wages of sin would sound as hypocritical as a sermon by a prosperous gambler on the evils of poker and faro. Wolf had been too successful; not only had he remained free for all these years but also he had accumulated enough wealth to buy a ranch and to retire if he wanted to. Talking would do little good, but he must try.

He prepared the turkey and put it into the oven, then went outside and busied himself about the place, returning to the cabin occasionally to turn and baste the roasting turkey. Dave slept like a hibernating bear.

About four o'clock he saw a rider racing toward the cabin from the direction of the ranch, and after a long look recognized Patricia Downing, granddaughter of Will Downing, his ranch manager.

He gave a grunt, but it was not a grunt of dislike. In his grudging way he liked Pat, although he was careful not to let her know this. Pat kept house for her grandfather and helped him and their three hands with the range work. Sixteen? Maybe eighteen; Wolf did not know.

She baked pies and cakes for him and fetched him fresh bread when he was at home; and when he was away she rode over and cleaned his cabin so that it was always neat when he returned. She had blue eyes that crinkled at the corners, sun-bleached brown hair, a dimple, and freckles on her nose.

She rode to where he stood, bounced out of the saddle and smiled at him. She carried a newspaper-wrapped bundle.

'I saw your smoke,' she said, 'and thought you'd like some fresh baked bread. Did you have a good trip, Uncle Chris?'

She had adopted him as Uncle Chris from the first.

He answered her shortly. 'Ran into bad luck. Had my herd rustled. Young fellow helping me on the drive was hit. He's asleep inside.'

The smile faded. 'Can I do anything? I'm pretty good at doctoring.'

'So am I. Besides, I told you, he's sleeping. Lost lots of blood and needs rest and plenty of good food.'

'We're having roast beef for supper. I could fetch some over.'

'Thanks. I'm roasting a turkey.'

'Oh!' She seemed disappointed. 'Can I take a

peep at him?'

'I guess so,' he said reluctantly. 'But be quiet.'

She went into the cabin and he followed her to the doorway. She tiptoed to the bunk and stood for a short while looking down at Dave. His face was pale but relaxed, his dark, damp hair curled above a sweaty forehead. She turned away, came quietly through the doorway.

'At least, there's no fever,' she said softly.

'I told you all he needs is rest and food. Thanks for the bread.'

It was a dismissal, but Pat did not appear to mind. There was a faraway look in her eyes and she said mechanically, 'You're welcome,' and got on her pony. She rode away, slowly at first, then spurring the pinto into a wild scamper. It would take nearly an hour of steady riding to reach the ranch house.

* * *

Wolf sat down on the bench outside the doorway and scowled after her. He concentrated once more on the problem presented by a son who wanted to go wrong and whom he wanted above everything else to go straight. He sat there until Pat became a dot and finally disappeared altogether, but no solution came to him, and finally the odor from the kitchen told him the turkey was nearly done.

He went inside and put the potatoes on the front of the stove. He had to feed the fire, and the rattle of iron stove lids awakened Dave. The boy sat up, ran lean fingers through the damp hair.

'How long have I been sleeping?' His voice was stronger.

Wolf told him. 'We'll eat as soon as the potatoes are done. How do you feel?'

'Better, but gosh-awful weak.' He continued irritably, 'How long do I have to be so helpless?'

'Until you get back the blood you lost. Takes time.'

'It can't be soon enough for me.' He gazed somberly at Wolf. 'I don't know how to thank you for what you've done for me.'

'Then don't.'

'I'll pay you back some day.'

Wolf silently turned his back, opened the oven and moved the rack forward to examine the turkey.

Dave went on: 'I was a stranger and you had nothing to lose by letting Ed Grant arrest me. You didn't; you got me away.'

Wolf pushed back the rack, slammed the oven door, turned to face him. 'I should have let him take you. A few days in jail and you would have been free. Might have gotten some of the fool kid notions out of your head. But as it is, you got plugged.'

'That was my fault for making a target of myself. I know better now. You should have left me when I was hit, and back there in the ravine you should have left me after you spotted the posse. You didn't; you stuck with me.'

'Don't be such a fool! Think what I did was for you? It wasn't. I did it to show Ed Grant I could beat him at any game he wants to play.'

'You've been showing him that for twenty years. No, that's not the reason. You did it because—' He broke off, made a helpless gesture. 'Oh, I don't know why you did it.' He leaned forward, his intent gaze on the outlaw. 'Wolf, I want to ride with you. From here right to the end of the line.'

'Nobody rides with me, least of all you.'

'Why? Why? You've never thrown in with anybody because you couldn't trust them. But you can trust me, Wolf, you know you can! I'd never cross you, even if it meant my life!'

'I don't want you with me. Get out of Ed Grant's territory; go back to Wyoming where you came from.'

The boy gave a short, bitter laugh. 'Go back to what? From the first my grandfather figured I was just another mouth to feed. He hated me. He put me to work as soon as I could sit a saddle, and never did give me a nickel's wages. I worked like a dog for my keep. I stuck it out because of Ma, then when she died I lit out.

Now I got nobody that I care a hoot about but you, and nobody cares a hoot about me. When I go back it'll be with more money in my jeans than the old man ever saw.'

'Then get a job and earn it. You ought to be a pretty good cowhand.'

'I am, but thirty bucks a month is too slow, much too slow. Grandpap will be under the clover before I'd be able to start a spread of my own. And I *got* to show him!' He waved his good arm in a fierce gesture that embraced the rolling range, the stock, the buildings. 'Look what you got! How long would it take me to get something like this? If I ride with you I can make a quick stake. I can go back and wave a bundle of banknotes in front of Grandpap's face that'll make him blink, and by the time you're ready to settle down and take it easy I'll have enough to buy my own brand.'

Wolf regarded him, scowling. It was not just that the boy wanted to emulate him, he was obsessed with the idea of showing his grandfather that he had succeeded despite the old man's efforts to pin him down. Dave believed his grandfather hated him. Well, perhaps he did; perhaps he was heaping on the boy the bitter resentment and humiliation piled on them by David's outlawed father. Success, quick success, was important to Dave; but the means of attaining it wasn't. All he wanted was money; lots of it, and fast.

Dave had sat up and swung his feet to the floor. Wolf walked over, drew a chair from beneath the table, turned its back to the bunk and straddled the seat, facing Dave.

'Son,' he said quietly, 'I'm going to talk to you like your father would, if you had one. What you want to do is natural enough; what ain't natural is the way you want to do it.'

'But you did it that way.'

'Yes; and God knows how many times I've cursed the day I made the mistake you want to make now.'

'Yeah? I'll bet you—'

Wolf cut in sharply. 'Shut up and let me talk. I bought this spread with money I stole. Much of the stock was stolen, too. One or two at a time, maybe more if driving them wasn't too tough. But every square foot of this land and every cow on it I paid for with my blood or days of misery and fear and heartache. I could have had twice what I have now if I had put the past twenty years of my life in honest work, instead of stealing and killing.

'It didn't take me long to realize that instead of being smart I was the biggest damn fool I knew, but by that time I couldn't quit. I'd killed, and there's no statute of limitations on that. There was nothing I could do but stick to the trail I'd taken and follow it to the end. That end is the one thing I'm sure of. It's death by a bullet or death by the rope. It's in the cards;

and that's the way it will be.'

He was silent for a little while, holding the boy with his steady, somber gaze. Dave gazed back unblinkingly. He did not appear to be greatly impressed. Wolf went on:

'You see only one side of the picture. You see a man who's done wrong for twenty years and got away with it. What you don't see are the things that made an old man of me when others are starting to enjoy life and take it easy.

'I hope you'll never know what it means to be hunted like a locoed wolf, always running or hiding, afraid to make friends for fear they'll betray you for the price on your head, afraid of every rock and bush because it might hide somebody itching to kill you, knowing that you won't even get the chance to surrender, because the bounty posters say "Dead or Alive." Even if you kill in self-defense, you're a murderer. You walk and ride looking over your shoulder, you go without food or sleep, and when you do close your eyes you have your hand on your gun and fear in your heart. You have to keep moving, using the money you stole to keep life in your body.'

'You've managed right well for twenty years.'

'Yeah. Folks call me lucky. But I'm not. I would have been luckier if they had killed me right after that first job. Many times I've wanted to turn back on the posse and go out in one big blaze of glory, but you want to know the truth? I didn't have the guts. Folks like you think I'm brave; they're crazy as hell! Everything I have I got the coward's way, stealing in the night, throwing a gun on some defenseless man and making him shell out. I just didn't have the guts to go out and earn it the honest way.'

'Why are you telling me this?' asked Dave coldly.

'Because I don't want to see a promising young feller like you throwing away his future for a few quick dollars.'

Dave shook his head. 'I can't swallow that, Wolf. There's no reason for you to show any interest in what I do or don't do. You told me this because you don't want to take me with you. You think I ain't good enough to be your partner. I am! Like I told you, I'm green, but I learn quick. And I'd never let you down. You understand that, don't you, Wolf? *I'd never let you down*!'

Wolf felt a deep pity and an even deeper futility. It had been no go; he had not really thought it would be. He made a despairing gesture and got up from the chair.

'Might as well eat,' he said shortly.

He was putting things on the table when they heard the brisk beat of hoofs. Wolf glided along the wall with that cougar-like tread, his hand on his gun. He peered around the door frame, then relaxed and stepped outside. A horse pulled up and Dave heard him call, 'What do you want?'

A woman's voice answered:

'I fetched over a pie, Uncle Chris. You said your sick man needed lots of good food. Here, take it; I've had to balance it on my hand all the way over.'

'Tie your pony and come in,' Wolf said gruffly.

He entered the cabin bearing a pie, which he set on the table. He went to the stove and started to dish out the food. The girl came into the room, halting just within the doorway.

Wolf said over his shoulder, 'Pat Downing, Dave. Granddaughter of the man who runs the ranch for me.'

Dave got up. 'Howdy, Miss Downing. I'm David Singleton.'

'Pleased to meet you, Mr. Singleton. You sit down. Uncle Chris told me you were hurt when the cattle you were driving were rustled.'

Wolf said quickly, 'He can sit down at the table. We're about to eat.'

He turned with the turkey, halted and flashed a keen glance at them. Dave was staring at Pat and she was staring at him. They seemed unable to see anything but each other.

Slowly the harshness went out of Wolf's face. He put the turkey on the table, drew up another chair, went to the cupboard and came back with a third plate and set of utensils.

'Sit down and eat with us, Pat,' he invited

with unusual cordiality.

She took her gaze from Dave. Her cheeks were flushed. 'Thanks, Uncle Chris. I really should rush back and get supper for Gramp.'

'That roast beef you told me about is in the oven. All Will's got to do is take it out and eat it. Come on; sit down.'

'Please do,' begged Dave.

'Well-l—' She made a sudden little gesture of acceptance and gave Dave a sunny smile. 'All right. I guess Gramp can shift for himself just this once.'

Dave almost jumped in his eagerness to draw out a chair for her.

When they had eaten, Pat told them to smoke while she cleared the table and washed the dishes. Wolf filled his pipe and sat in the armchair with the rawhide seat, and Dave helped Pat remove the dishes from the table.

'I can do it,' she told him. 'You should rest.'

'I'm tired of resting. That supper put me right back on my feet.'

She washed the dishes and he wiped them, while Wolf sat and smoked and felt pretty good. Perhaps the solution of his problem was in the making, he thought. Let a handsome, healthy young fellow like his son Dave fall in love with a girl like Pat, and a life of being on the dodge might lose some of its appeal.

He felt rested and comfortable. This was it. This would turn the trick!

CHAPTER FIVE

'I've got to run now,' said Pat when she had hung the dish towel on the line behind the stove. 'Gramp will be sending out a searching party.'

'I'll ride over with you.'

She shook her head, smiling. 'It's ten miles over and back, and you're a little shaky right now. Next time, maybe.'

'You're sure there'll be a next time?'

'Of course. I ride over quite often, don't I, Uncle Chris?'

'Couldn't get along without you,' lied Wolf tranquilly.

Dave went outside with her and held her horse while she mounted. Wolf smoked and grinned. Pat needed help in mounting about as much as a bird needs help in flying. Their voices reached him.

'Mind if I come over to see you sometime?'

'I wish you would. I want you to meet Gramp. You'll like him. And the hills are very pretty on our side of the basin. I've played around in them ever since I could ride. If you'd like me to, I'll show you some of the country.'

'I'd like that, I sure would! I'll be over in a day or two. But,' he added hastily, 'don't wait for me. You come over again as soon as you can.'

'Maybe I'll fetch another pie.'

'You sure do make them good. Just like my mother used to.'

'Your mother—she's dead?'

'Yes.'

'I'm sorry, David. I lost both my parents when I was very small. Gramp is all I have ... Well, good-by.'

'Good-by. You come over, now.'

'I will.'

She rode over to the doorway, called, 'Good-by, Uncle Chris. It was a wonderful supper.'

He called a farewell and she rode away, turning in the saddle to wave to Dave. He stood watching until she crossed a ridge, then came slowly into the cabin.

Wolf said, 'You'd better lie down a spell. You're sort of wobbly.'

Dave stretched out on the bunk, locked his hands behind his head and stared at the ceiling. Wolf guessed that it was not the ceiling he saw, but a girl with sunburned brown hair, freckles, and a dimple. But he said nothing; he did not want to crowd his luck.

The next morning, Dave, his strength returning quickly, helped Wolf with the chores. After dinner he saddled his horse and rode for a short distance into the hills. He returned looking quite fit and with color in his cheeks, but Wolf made him lie down and have his wound dressed, then told him to stay on the bunk and rest.

Around four o'clock, Dave got up and went outside, but returned almost at once. 'She's coming!' he grinned.

'Who?'

'Pat. Who did you think?'

'Oh, her!'

Dave went outside to meet her, and Wolf heard her say, 'I fetched over another pie. Plenty of good, rich food, you know.'

'That sure is nice of you. You'll stay and help eat it, won't you?'

'Not today. Gramp finished up the roast and now he's howling for steak. I'll just say hello to Uncle Chris and run. How are you feeling?'

'Great. All right if I ride over tomorrow?'

'Sure. Gramp's right anxious to meet you.'

She came into the cabin, Dave following her with the pie. They chatted briefly, then she left for home with a renewed promise by Dave to visit the ranch the next day. When they had cleaned up the supper dishes, Wolf and Dave settled down to a game of cassino, but the boy's mind was not on the cards and they turned in early.

Dave made himself useful outside the next morning repairing the pole corral and patching the roof of the open shed which sheltered the buckboard and their rigs. After dinner he scrubbed, put on his clean shirt, brushed his clothes and set out for the ranch.

Wolf lighted his pipe and sat on the bench outside the doorway. His eyes were warm as he watched the disappearing back of his son. He could not get over the wonder of it; this big, handsome young man was his own flesh and blood, and knowing it made him proud and happy.

He felt younger and the burden of fear had lifted. It was in the cards, he told himself, that Dave would fall in love with Pat and she with him. They'd marry, and Wolf would make him ranch foreman. When Wolf reached the end of the trail, then they'd have the ranch for themselves.

He finished his smoke, knocked out his pipe on the edge of the bench, and went into the cabin. He got on a chair, reached over the top log of the east wall and drew out a metal box. He opened it, took out some money and estimated the amount remaining. The treasury needed replenishing, especially so now that there were two of them.

He had gone to the saloon where he had met Dave with the intention of holding up the place around closing time when there would be a maximum of cash on the tables and in the till, but Dave's adventure in crime had cancelled this out, and now he must pull a job somewhere else. He would have to find an excuse to keep

Dave in the basin while he was away. Perhaps Pat would help.

He replaced the box, went outside and saddled his horse to the buckboard. Supplies were low and now was as good a time as any to drive to Santa Anita and restock. Juan Mendoza's store was small and the selection limited, but the fact that it was here and called for an hour's drive instead of the good day's journey to Briscoe was the decisive factor.

Santa Anita was a very small settlement, but the houses had been scattered about without regard to pattern or symmetry and so wide apart that the one street stretched for half a mile. Mendoza's store, larger than any of the other buildings, was located about halfway up the street; across from it was Felipe Pacheco's cantina.

Wolf noticed two things as he wheeled the buckboard into the crooked street. The first was the total absence of human beings. This was disturbing, for it was the custom of some of the Mexicans to take their siesta in what shade they could find, backs against a wall, knees drawn up and sombreros pulled down.

He noticed another thing as his gaze went up the street. A saddled horse stood outside the store and he knew by the rig that it did not belong to any of the native Mexicans. It could belong to a cowboy from one of the outlying ranches, but such a visitor would not explain the absence of somnolent *paisanos*.

He turned the horse abruptly off the street and halted him beside a *jacal* where animal and buckboard could not be seen from the store. A paneless window yawned at him, the interior of the house made more gloomy by contrast with the bright sunlight outside. Wolf got down from the seat and called softly through the window.

'This is Chris Jones. Whose horse is that down at the store?'

A brown face materialized and a woman's voice, sharp with excitement, answered: 'It is that of a robber, senor! He has a cloth over his face and a gun in his hand. He goes into the store and we come inside and bar the doors!'

Wolf dropped the lines in front of the horse and strode to the back of the hut and around it. He ran toward the store, dodging around the scattered houses. He had raided many a store himself, but this was different. Mendoza's store was the only one within forty miles and Wolf and his ranch were dependent upon it for supplies. In a sense, it was one of his pet interests; just as there was never a *baile*, a wedding or christening that he was not invited to—almost every boy and girl there, up to the age of twelve, was his godchild . . . The store, like the rest of the town, must be preserved and protected.

He circled so as to approach the store from

the rear. He vaulted to the loading platform, tried the back door, found it unbarred. He went into a small back room where Mendoza kept his surplus stock and closed the door behind him.

There were no windows in this room, but a double width doorway led to the store proper. The pleading voice of old Ysidro Mendoza reached him.

'Senor, you have taken all! I have no money hid away. I swear it!'

Wolf heard the thud of fist on flesh, the old man's agonized cry.

'You lie! You're the richest man in town; you must have more. You'll tell me where it is, or do I put a slug between your eyes and find it myself?'

'Senor, I swear there is nothing more!'

'Shut up!' Another thud, another cry of pain. 'I ain't got all day. I'll count to three and that's all. *One*!'

Wolf glided to the connecting doorway, his .45 in his hand. Old Mendoza cringed against the counter, his seamed face twisted, his clawlike hands held half in supplication, half in protection, before his face. His left eye was swollen almost shut, there was a cut on his cheek and blood on his lips.

Before him towered a big, heavy man, shabbily dressed, with a bandanna covering his face from the eyes down. The man had twisted the fingers of his left hand in Mendoza's shirt and his right fist was cocked threateningly. His gun was in its holster. Neither he nor Mendoza had heard or seen Wolf come to the doorway.

'*Two!*' said the big man, and put his hand on the butt of his gun.

'Two's enough,' said Wolf.

There was complete lack of sound or movement for perhaps five seconds; then Mendoza's head swiveled on his skinny neck and relief came into his good eye. '*Senor Jones!*'

The big man turned his head slowly and Wolf recognized him. With recognition came a sudden red rage. He was a petty cowthief and small-time holdup artist who called himself Texas Jack, and Wolf had been hoping to run into him for more than six months.

Texas Jack recognized Wolf also, but knew nothing about his rage. He let go Mendoza's shirt and carefully removed his hand from the butt of his Colt.

'You, huh? "Senor Jones," is it? What's the matter, am I hornin' in on your territory?'

'Give that money back.'

Wolf's voice was sharp with menace and his .45 was pointed at Texas Jack's belly.

'Sure, sure. I didn't know—'

Texas Jack put a hand into a pocket, drew forth a handful of coins and bills. He put them on the counter, fished into the pocket again and brought out the rest.

Wolf asked, his gaze steady on Texas Jack,

'That all of it, *viejo*?'

'*Si, patron*. He puts it only in the one pocket.'

'Go to your house and have your good Luz patch up your face.'

Mendoza scooped up the money and scurried through the doorway.

Wolf said, 'Back up five steps, Jack.'

Texas Jack took the five paces and stopped. 'I don't get it, Wolf!'

'You will. I've been looking for you, Jack; looking everywhere for you. Remember Ben Miller?'

He saw the reaction in Jack's eyes. The eyelids flickered slightly and that was all.

'Never heard of him.'

'You lie! You knew him in Briscoe. He tipped Ed Grant off that I was in town and Ed laid a trap for me. I got a bullet through the chest on that little deal, and came near cashing in my chips.'

'I don't know nothing about that.'

'You lie again! I tracked Ben down. I was all set to kill him when he shouted that he had been hired to turn me in. I traded his life for the name of the man who hired him. He named you.'

'He lied to save his skin! I tell you, I don't!'

'Shut up! Ben could have named any one of a hundred men in Briscoe, but he named the only one who had seen me without my mustache and recognized me.'

He slipped the .45 into its holster, fell into a slight crouch, elbow crooked, fingers clawed. 'Drag your iron!'

'No! No, Wolf! I swear to God—!'

'Draw, you mangy skunk! Go on—*draw*!'

Jack pushed his hands into the air in a frantic gesture of surrender. 'I don't stand a chance against you, Wolf! It would be murder!'

'You'll damned well wish it was!'

Wolf leaped forward, drawing the Colt as he did so. Three long strides brought him close to Texas Jack. He seized the end of the bandanna and jerked and the mask came down. He raised the gun, turned it, brought it down in a vicious rake along Jake's left cheek. The front sight caught Jack just below the temple and ripped a gash from eye corner to chin. Texas Jack had been pistol whipped, the most degrading punishment that can be handed out. He would wear Wolf's brand to his grave.

He staggered backward, crying out in pain and anger, but he did not try to draw his gun. His hand went up to cover the wound and blood oozed between his fingers.

Wolf made a gesture. 'Get out! And if you ever see me again, start running!'

Jack turned and staggered along the aisle. At the door, he pulled the bandanna up over the bridge of his nose, more to conceal the degrading mark than to hide his identity. He stumbled to his horse and pulled himself into the saddle, and when Wolf reached the doorway his horse was kicking up dust in frantic flight.

Wolf pushed the Colt into its holster and strode across the street to Pacheco's cantina. There was nobody in the place, but when he shouted the man's name, Felipe opened a door and came into the room.

'You chased the *bandido* away?'

'I chased him away. How about a drink?'

'But of a certainty, Senor Christofero! The very best! And is on the 'ouse.'

CHAPTER SIX

With the swift departure of Texas Jack, Santa Anita came alive. Men and women spilled out of their *jacales*, the former hurrying to Pacheco's cantina, the latter forming an animated cluster to chatter in shrill, excited voices. Old Mendoza came from his house, face crisscrossed with court plaster applied by his white-haired wife with the dancing black eyes, and holding a piece of raw beef to the blackening eye, to join the men in the cantina.

To his annoyance, Senor Jones found himself a hero. He had tried to remain as unobtrusive as possible and up until now had succeeded. He got away as quickly as he could by reminding Mendoza that he had come to town to buy supplies.

Mendoza quickly made up the list and waved aside the payment Wolf tendered. 'You owe me nothing, *patron*. It is I who owe you.'

'You don't owe me a damned thing,' grinned Wolf. 'The man who held you up is a personal enemy, Ysidro, and I would have jumped him no matter where I found him.' After the usual flowery exchange of amenities in the Mexican language, Wolf convinced Ysidro that he would be doing Wolf a great favor by taking the money.

He shouldered his box of groceries and left the store. Up the crooked street he went, passing the knot of grinning, admiring women, put the box in the back of the buckboard and set out for home.

He took stock as he drove, scowling at the horse's ears. He had wanted to kill Texas Jack, who undoubtedly deserved killing, and he wondered now why he had let the man go. Ordinarily he would have given Texas Jack the chance to draw, and if he was too chicken-hearted to fight for his life, would have let him have it, anyhow, so long as Jack was armed. But for some reason he hadn't done this, and now there would be complications.

While he lived, Texas Jack was a stupendous liability. He wanted the five thousand dollars' reward that had been named as the price on Wolf's scalp, and now to greed would be added a vicious hatred. Jack knew him now as Senor Jones and would surely learn that he owned a ranch in the basin. Jack would lose no time in seeing to it that word reached Ed Grant and the hideaway which Wolf had so carefully selected might become his death-trap. He could have shot Texas Jack through the head without any questions being asked, and without the slightest compunction, because he had caught Jack in the act of armed robbery, and beating an all-but-helpless old man. But, for some strange reason, he hadn't. He was halfway home before it occurred to him that he had acted as he did because of his son, David. Somewhere deep within his subconscious had been born the desire to do things as he would have David do them, and shooting down a man who was too cowardly to use his defenses, was not one of them.

He was getting soft, he told himself fiercely, and the least bit of softness might bring about complete disaster. He must kill Texas Jack to preserve his own safety, and if it was at all possible he must do it at once.

He jerked erect and slapped the reins against the horse's rump, putting the animal to a run. At the cabin, he quickly unharnessed and got into a pair of bullhide chaps and buckled on his spurs. He carried the box of groceries into the house and wrote a brief note, leaving it on the table where Dave would surely see it. He simply said that he had been called away on business, and that Dave should stick at the cabin while he was gone.

He packed some grub in his saddlebags and set out toward Santa Anita. Bypassing the town, he cut back into the wagon road a mile or so beyond. He followed the fresh prints of Jack's horse for some distance, then left the road when they did and plunged into the undergrowth at the foot of the hills. For some time he followed the trail of broken brush, then reached a rocky flat and lost the trail altogether. He rode to the far end of the flat without picking up sign and began casting about in a zigzag course, realizing the immensity of the country and the multitude of hiding places it offered. Darkness came and he made dry camp for the night.

He went at it again as soon as it was daylight, but as the minutes went by realization of the futility of a one-man search reached him. Then there was David. Suppose the boy concluded from his brief note that he had gone on another job? He was suddenly apprehensive and fearful; he had taken twenty years to find his son, he must not lose him now.

At noon he turned back.

When he reached the cabin late that afternoon he found Dave seated on the bench waiting for him. He waved a hand and rode around to the corral, and Dave got up and followed him. Wolf off-saddled and Dave led the horse to the corral. They walked to the house together.

Wolf said, 'Time to get supper. You eat with the Downings last night?'

'Yes.'

'See Pat today?'

'Rode over this morning just long enough to tell her you had gone away and I had to stick around the cabin. I met her grandfather while I was there.'

'What do you think of Will Downing?'

'He's all right. Said he was aiming to talk to you about hiring another hand. Offered me the job, if you told him to go ahead.'

They were in the cabin and Wolf was breaking kindling for the fire. 'What did you say to that?'

'Told him I was already working for you.'

'News to me. When did I hire you on?'

'I hired myself.'

Wolf put a match to the kindling, fanned the flames with his hat. 'Just remember that when payday comes around.'

'I don't want any pay. I want to ride with you, pay my own way. I want to do that more than I want anything else.'

Wolf turned to eye him cynically. 'More than you want Pat Downing?'

Dave's face tightened. He did not shift his gaze. 'Of course. We're just friends.'

It was not the answer Wolf had hoped for and

it angered him. 'You're not riding with me, and that's flat and final,' he grated. 'I don't want a kid that ain't dry behind the ears tagging along with me.'

He saw color rise in Dave's cheeks. 'I said that was the reason why you won't take me with you. I'm green; you don't know how I'll act when the pressure is on. All right; I'll prove what I can do. Give me a job, a one-man job. You won't be mixed up in it. Just tell me what to do, and I'll show you.'

'You'll do no such fool thing as that!' Wolf bit off the words. 'This is my hide-out, the only place where I'm safe. You do anything to draw attention to this basin and I'll peel off your hide and beat you with it!'

They were glaring at each other, but the boy's gaze did not waver.

'You hear me, Dave? You'll walk the straight and narrow as long as I have anything to do with it.'

For a few seconds Dave continued to return Wolf's glare; then he let out his breath and shifted his gaze. 'All right. Forget it.'

But Wolf knew that Dave would not forget it. The boy honestly believed that Wolf was afraid his inexperience would get them both into trouble; indeed, there was nothing else for him to believe. In an effort to prove that he was worthy of the partnership, Dave would attempt something on his own when he got the chance.

Wolf must see to it that he did not get the chance.

They were eating supper when Dave casually asked, 'How'd you make out with your—business?'

'I didn't.'

Dave was silent for a short space, then he said, 'You don't have to tell me, of course; but I'd like to feel that you trust me.'

'It wasn't what you think it was. I was looking for a man I know is somewhere in this part of the country. I didn't find him.'

The boy asked no more questions, but Wolf knew that he did not believe him.

The next morning, Wolf kept Dave busy about the place, cleaning up, making minor repairs; in fact, killing time. What to do was a problem, and Wolf was restless and disturbed. Menace hung over him like a miasmic cloud. And the cash box must soon be refilled.

Pat rode over that afternoon and coaxed Dave to go for a ride to Santa Anita. 'We need a few things, not enough to use the wagon, and I thought you might want to go along.'

Dave looked questioningly at Wolf, and Wolf said, 'Go ahead; I don't need you right now.'

They rode away together, and once more Wolf lighted his pipe and seated himself on the bench to think things over.

So far as Ed Grant was concerned, all he could do was remain vigilant. He would have a week or so of grace, for Texas Jack would hardly appear in public until his cut cheek had partly mended. It would take him some time to locate Ed, and even then he must find somebody to do the dirty work, since Ed was also anxious to lay hands on him.

Meanwhile, what to do about Dave? Pat would keep him busy part of the time, but he must find something to keep him occupied when he was home. But whatever he dreamed up would be but a stopgap and entirely inadequate.

No matter how he figured it, there seemed no solidly satisfactory solution. He was a hunted man and might have to light out fast at any moment. In that case, Dave would insist on going with him, pointing out that he was wanted, too. Wolf could not very well refuse. The boy had no friends but Pat and himself, and—except for the little he had taken from the gambler—no money. If Wolf left him, he'd strike out on his own in an attempt to convince Wolf of his worth, and might be caught or killed. If he tried to pull a job himself and succeeded, there'd be no stopping him. He had a bad case of El Lobo-itis.

He thought of deeding the ranch over to Dave with the excuse that he had to leave the country and could not look after it. If Dave refused the ranch as a gift, as he probably would, Wolf would tell him he could pay for it from the profits. In time, the boy-and-girl friendship between Dave and Pat would become love, and with a wife to support and the means of supporting her right here in the basin, Dave might stay put. Wolf would visit them from time to time, and . . .

He broke the thought, frowning. Here he was, falling into the same trap that had snared many an outlaw. Once Ed Grant knew that he hung out here, Ed would keep the place constantly covered. Just the same, now that he had found his son, nothing would prevent his enjoying the boy's company as long and as often as he possibly could.

Meanwhile, the cash box . . .

There was Jupiter, a hundred miles or so to the east. No bank, but there had been a gold strike and Mike Maloney's antiquated safe was a repository for dust and nuggets and freshly minted coins. Wolf had visited the place and had put it on his list of prospects. If the haul was as big as he expected it to be, he could lay off for many months to come.

He would have to take another business trip, and Dave must be left behind. He wouldn't like it, but he'd have to lump it. Wolf got up and went into the cabin to lie on his bunk and plan just how to relieve Mike Maloney of his riches . . .

* * *

Even if Wolf had persisted in his search for Texas Jack, it is doubtful if he would have found the camp at the bottom of a deep ravine where the outlaw was hiding out. It was an ideal spot, a tiny oasis in a desert of hills, with a small stream and patches of grass where his horse could graze. An overhanging ledge shielded him from sun and rain, and the smoke from his cooking fire was dissipated before it reached the summits of the steep rock walls on both sides. The ravine was but one of many that gouged the terrain, and one literally had to stumble into it to find the camp.

He sat on a stone beneath the ledge staring fiercely at the trickle of water in the ravine bed and nursing the fierce hatred that only the coward can know. Slanting downward on his left cheek was a line of court plaster. He had drawn the clean edges of the cut together as closely as he could and had anchored them with the plaster; but he knew this dressing was inadequate. The cut should have been stitched up by a doctor, but the nearest doctor was at Briscoe, and in any event he did not have the courage to face a doctor who would know immediately what had caused such a cut.

He had carried the slash around with him for a full day, and his hatred for El Lobo had intensified by the hour. Mixed with hatred was a sense of futility. This pistol-whipping was an insult to his manhood and he must avenge it, but other men had matched wits and guns with El Lobo and had finished a poor second.

The one sure way was to get Wolf from ambush, but in that case he would lose the five thousand dollars that had been offered for the outlaw, dead or alive, for the simple reason that he could not collect it from the sheriff without putting his own neck in a noose. He could get word to Ed Grant where El Lobo was hiding out, but the ultimate result would be even more unsatisfactory because Ed would do the killing and collect the reward. He had tried using a confederate, the reward to be split between them, but see what had happened! He fingered the court plaster and the scowl grew blacker.

But no matter what he eventually did, the first thing to do was to locate the exact place where Wolf was hiding out. He could learn this at Santa Anita, and if he went to that town on a Saturday, when the ranchers came in to do their trading and cowboys to do their drinking and gambling, he was sure he would not be recognized.

The storekeeper had been the only one to see him at close range, and then he was masked and wearing the shabby clothes he always wore when pulling a job. The slash on his cheek was a dead giveaway, but nobody knew about that but Wolf, who was not given to bragging about his victories. He was pretty sure Wolf had told nobody about it. If he had, the first look on a Mexican face would tip him off. He would wear a wider bandage and explain that the cut had been made by a knife. There was no disgrace in carrying a knife wound, for that at least implied the courage of a hand-to-hand fight.

He nodded and let the scowl fade. Take things one at a time, Jack, he told himself. Find first where Wolf holed up, and a way to do the rest would come . . .

CHAPTER SEVEN

Dave returned to the cabin when Wolf was eating supper. He left his horse standing and came right in.

'Thought you'd eat with the Downings,' said Wolf.

'They asked me to, but I came right home.' His eyes were bright, and Wolf saw he was trying to keep his excitement under control. 'Wolf, the storekeeper told me how you saved him from a holdup. Sounded sort of crazy to me at first, you stopping a holdup, but then I got it. We can't let anybody put *that* store out of business, can we?'

'What do you mean, "we?" I know the cheap holdup and I don't like him, so I ran him off. Besides, Mendoza and all those people there are my friends . . . Put up your horse and get some hot grub off the stove.'

Dave went outside and took care of his horse, and while he was doing this, Wolf dished up food for him. Dave came in, sat down and started to eat.

Wolf asked, 'Why didn't you eat with the Downings? Pat's attraction wearing off already?'

'No. I—Well, I don't want to wear out my welcome. And I wanted to see you and hear about it. Did you run him off with a gun?'

'Oh, hell! I stamped my foot and said "*scat*," and he scatted.'

'I'll bet!' Dave's eyes were shining.

'Look!' said Wolf sharply. 'Get it out of your head that I'm someone who's big and brave; a—a sort of Robin Hood, that I used to read about when I was a kid. I'm not any of those things. I'm in this game because there's nothing else left for me. I told you that before. Believe it. Anybody who takes up killing and stealing by choice is weak in the head, and at least a moral coward, to boot. That's me, weak in the head, and a coward, too. For God's sake get this dream of quick and easy money out of your mind. Take a job with Downing and stick to it. Marry Pat and settle down to raising cattle and kids, and don't carry the fear of a rope or bullet with you all the rest of your life.'

David, a forkful of food half raised, gazed

wonderingly at him. 'Wolf, I don't get you at all. You've succeeded at this game. I bet if you had it to do over, you'd do it again.'

'No, by God!'

'Oh, yes you would! You were cut out for it. Working for a ranch-hand's wages—what's that?' He put down the fork, spoke vehemently. 'Branding in a hot corral in the summer, freezing to death in the winter keeping the stock fed and moving, tailing up bogged-down critters, digging post holes and stringing fence, riding circle at roundup until you're ready to fall off your horse, eating dust in the drag on a slow drive—and all for thirty a month! No, Wolf, that's not for you and it's not for me.' He looked at Wolf hopefully. 'When do you pull off the next job?'

'For hell's sake!' Wolf cried furiously, and threw down his knife.

'Now don't get mad. You think I'm not up to it. Then, I'll wait until I am. I'll wait a long time, but one of these days you'll say, "Well, you might as well tag along," and then I'll show you!'

Wolf's appetite was gone. He got up from the table, angrily stuffed his pipe, lighted it. He sat down in the rawhide rocker and puffed for several minutes. David resumed his eating.

'Look,' said Wolf at last. 'I've got something for you that'll pay off a damned sight better than holding up banks and trains. That man I chased out of Santa Anita, he knows me. He heard Mendoza call me Senor Jones, and he'll find out that I own a ranch in the basin, or anyway hang out here. He'll get word to Ed Grant and I'll have to cut for it. If I keep the ranch, you can bet he'll have it covered forever on the chance of catching me here. So I'm going to deed the ranch over to you, and if you run it right, you'll make money.'

'Wolf, have you gone crazy?'

'No. I've got to unload. What good is a ranch to me if I can't ever come near it? I've got nobody else to leave it to. Dammit, do me a favor and take it off my hands!'

Dave sat, knife in one hand, fork in the other, gazing at him. 'You'd *give* it to me? You've known me less than a week and you'd *give* it to me?'

'It doesn't mean anything to me any more.'

'But why me? Why not Downing?'

'I have my reasons.'

The boy's face tightened. 'Sure you have! You're so scared that if you take me on a job with you I'll bungle the thing and get you killed—so damned scared that you'd give me your ranch to keep from taking me! Well, I don't want it. Even if that wasn't the reason, I'd never take it! Why, you can sell it for twenty, thirty thousand dollars cash! After all you've done for me, I wouldn't take it if it was gold-plated six inches thick! I—I just couldn't!'

Wolf made a scornful gesture. 'What good is twenty or thirty thousand dollars to me now?'

'You could take it and live like a lord in Mexico or South America. Europe, even.'

'I don't like Mexico and I don't like South America and I wouldn't be found dead in Europe. This is my country. I was born here and I'll die here. My God, boy, don't turn this chance down!'

Dave laid down knife and fork and got up slowly. He came over to the chair, his intent gaze on the older man. 'Wolf, I can't figure why you're doing this, but I'll take no more charity from you. I'll pay my own way through life, make my own living, not have it handed to me by a well-meaning but stubborn cuss like you.'

'It won't be a gift,' said Wolf desperately. 'You'll pay me for it every cent it's worth out of the profits.'

'I still call it charity. No man with any sense would make an offer like that to anybody, unless maybe it was his son. I've got thirteen dollars and a few cents I took from that gambler, and that's all. You don't know what I can do, or how well I can do it. I could run that ranch into the ground a lot quicker than I could build it up. Let me get the money I want my way. Take me along with you on a big job—a Wells-Fargo job. You know the ropes; you've done it alone. With me to help, even if it's just keeping the train crew covered, it would be a lot easier. One good haul would do it. A couple good ones and I could pay cash for the ranch, if you still wanted to get rid of it.'

Wolf shook his head. 'We do it my way or not at all.'

'Why,' asked Dave despairingly, 'can't you trust me? Why do you think I'm too dumb to learn?'

'It's not that. I do trust you or I wouldn't offer to sell you my ranch on the terms I made.' He lowered his voice, spoke earnestly. 'Take my offer, I can't unload the ranch in the open market now that Senor Jones is known to be El Lobo.'

'Will Downing can sell it for you. Give him power of attorney, or something.'

'I'd rather let you have it on time. Like I said, I couldn't spend the cash if I had it. Not usefully.'

'Wolf, I don't want it.'

'Then manage it for me. Split the profits.'

'Will Downing is a good manager. He's forgot more about cows than I'll ever know.'

'Then be my foreman. A hundred a month and found. Month in and month out, as regular as day and night. That's more than you'll average in a lifetime of holdups.'

Dave continued to watch him, and now Wolf saw bleakness come into his eyes. The boy turned away, went outside into the darkness. He was gone a long time and when he came in he started undressing.

'It's early,' said Wolf. 'How about a game of cassino?'

'No. I'm tired. I'm turning in.'

Wolf sat there smoking glumly. He had tried, and he had failed. Dave thought he was being offered the ranch in order that Wolf could avoid taking him as a partner. Hell, what else could he think? His offer had made the boy even more resentful.

He turned in at last, but he did not sleep. He couldn't. He lay quietly, breathing regularly, thinking, his eyes wide open. An hour passed.

It was dark in the cabin, but Dave's bunk was under a window, and Wolf saw him against the outside starlight as he sat quietly up in his bed. He sat there for fully five minutes and Wolf knew that he was looking across the room, listening. There was no sound as he lowered his feet to the floor and started dressing. There came a slight scrape as he picked up his boots. He moved quickly toward the door.

'Where are you going?'

Wolf came out of his bunk. He could not see Dave because the front door was closed. The answer came out of the darkness. 'I couldn't sleep.'

Wolf struck a match, lighted the lamp on the table. Dave, fully dressed except for his boots, which he carried, was half-way to the door. On the table beside the lamp lay thirteen dollars and a bit of paper. Wolf glanced at the paper, read:

You don't need me here, so I'm going. Thanks for everything.

Wolf felt a strange constriction in his throat that kept him from speaking for a moment. He killed time by rereading the note, then looked up at Dave.

'So you're running out on me!'

'I'm as well as I'll ever be.' The bleakness was still in Dave's eyes. 'There's no reason for my hanging around. There ain't enough to do to pay for my keep and I've got to find something to do sooner or later.'

'I offered you something to do—owner, manager, foreman. If you think that's charity, take the job of cowhand that Downing offered you.'

'No, Wolf. I told you that kind of job's not for me.'

'Then work for me. I need you. There's lots of things to do and I can't do them alone.'

'Wolf, there ain't a thing, and you know it.'

'I don't know it! Damn it, Dave, I'd planned to build me a real house instead of this shack.' It was the best he could think of at the moment. 'I want a log house with four rooms. I'll have to cut timber and saw it out. Take months.'

Dave regarded him doubtfully. 'You just said

you were going to unload.'

'The ranch, yes. But I got to keep this.' He sought desperately for a reason, found one. 'If I sell out, the Downings will have to be taken care of. I'll hold onto this quarter-section and turn it over to them. It's the least I can do. Stay and help me, son. I need you; I really do! Regular wages and keep.'

Dave considered, his doubtful gaze on Wolf. 'If I stay there'll be no wages. I'll help you for my keep.'

'But you will stay?'

'As long as you really need me. But no more charity, Wolf.'

'Thanks, son! Peel off your clothes and get back in bed.'

'I'll put up my horse first.'

He went out, and Wolf sat down on the bunk. He was sweating slightly. So that is what Dave had been doing when he left the cabin that evening—saddling his horse. The boy had become convinced that Wolf did not want his company, had made his triple offer merely to get rid of him.

Dave came back into the cabin. The bleakness was gone and he seemed happy. 'It's still early,' he said. 'How about a game of cassino?'

Wolf put on his pants and pulled a chair up to the table. They played, laughing and talking. They planned the house as they played, not caring who won or lost. If Ed Grant had walked in on them then, he would have had an easy time of it.

It was well after midnight when they went to bed, and as he was about to blow out the light, Wolf looked down on the little pile of coins and bills. 'You would have gone away without a cent.'

'I figured I owed it to you.'

'Put it back in your pocket and never insult me like that again.'

Both felt warm inside. The bond between them had been strengthened by the knowledge that each had come near losing the other.

They began work next day. With stakes and chalk line they marked the walls of the house, the partitions and doorways, making occasional changes as they talked it over, pooling their ideas. They exchanged banter and Wolf laughed along with Dave. Like father and son. But Dave noticed that Wolf never relaxed his vigilance. He had fetched a pair of binoculars with him and used them at regular intervals, searching the wooded slopes and distant hills. When they had placed their stakes to their satisfaction, Dave rode to the ranch to borrow another axe and a crosscut saw while Wolf rode to Santa Anita to buy an adze.

Money; he'd have to have some quickly. They would need milled lumber for floors and partitions, door and window frames; glass, hardware. For this house, Wolf decided, would be the best house that could be built. Some day Dave and Pat would occupy it, and he would build it so that other rooms could be added as their family grew. He must pull that Jupiter job and do it in such a way that Dave would not suspect. For he knew that he had not shaken the boy's determination to ride the outlaw trail with him.

That afternoon they went into the hills with their axes and two-handled crosscut saw. Wolf took the binoculars with him. From their elevation they had a good view of the basin, and with the glasses a rider could be identified at a distance of several miles. They felled several trees of the right diameter, trimmed them and cut them to length, snaking the logs to the site of the house with their ropes. It was late when they finished supper and they were tired, so they turned in early.

As they were undressing, Wolf said casually, 'You'll have to get along without me for a few days.'

'Yeah?' Dave put down a boot and stared at him. 'More business?'

'Business. We're going to need milled lumber and there's no sawmill nearby. It will have to be freighted in, so I'll have to order it ahead.'

'I see.' David resumed undressing, satisfied with the explanation. 'When are you going?'

'In the morning. I don't know if we can get

what we want in Briscoe or not. May have to go farther. Tomorrow's Friday; I'll try to get back some time Monday. Do what you can without me, but take Saturday off. Have Sunday dinner with the Downings; Pat always has something special on Sundays.'

They had an early breakfast and Wolf rode off as soon as the sun was up. As he swung into the saddle, Dave asked, 'You'll try Briscoe first?'

'Yes. It's the nearest big town. If I don't find what I want there I'll push on east to Mustang.'

Dave watched him ride off, then went into the house and got the binoculars and slung them over a shoulder. He rigged his horse, lashed the axe to the saddle and set out for the hills. Wolf was still in sight, a speck on the eastern horizon. He was following the stage road from Santa Anita. Pat had pointed it out to Dave when they were riding in the hills on the far side of the basin.

Dave climbed to where they had felled a tree, dismounted and tied his horse, then looked out into the basin. He saw a tiny dot that he knew must be Wolf and looked at it through the glasses. He made an adjustment in focus and saw that the rider was indeed Wolf. He could see the thin thread of road leading eastward towards Briscoe, and he could see the fork Pat had told him travelers took when they were heading for Jupiter, a hundred miles to the west. It passed through a gap Wolf was approaching and ran along the other side of the hills on the south side of the basin. Wolf, of course, would keep straight on.

Dave watched, enjoying the power of the binoculars. Wolf reached the gap and halted the horse. He turned in the saddle and sat for a full minute scanning his back trail. Cautious as always, thought Dave. I'll watch what he does and tell him when he comes home. It will puzzle him how I knew it until he thinks of the glasses.

He had not anticipated Wolf's next move at all. Satisfied that he was not being followed, Wolf swung his horse to the right and cut into the fork which led through the gap, the road one would follow in going to Jupiter. The gap swallowed him and he was lost to sight.

Dave continued to watch for some minutes, realizing that something might have attracted Wolf's attention and had drawn him off the Briscoe road; but he did not return, and Dave finally realized that instead of going to Briscoe, Wolf was going to Jupiter.

He did not want to believe that Wolf had lied to him, but there was a way of making sure. He got on his horse and rode into the basin. He raced the animal across the range and into the hills on the far side. It was a long ride crossing the hills, but Wolf had even farther to go. Dave found a place where he could see the road leading to the west and sat for half an hour waiting; then he saw movement on the road and trained the binoculars on a rider who was approaching from the east.

It was Wolf, and he was raising the dust, heading westward as fast as his horse could travel. The road was less than a mile from Dave and he knew he was not mistaken. Wolf was not going to Briscoe; must never have intended going there. He was heading for Jupiter, and Dave was certain that the business on which he was bent had nothing to do with milled lumber . . .

CHAPTER EIGHT

Dave rode back across the basin and went to work trimming the tree. He worked doggedly, driving himself. Wolf had lied to him. He was going on a holdup of some kind and he was going alone. Dave slashed angrily at a branch, the axe glanced off and flew out of his hands. He walked after it, snatched it up fiercely.

What else could he expect, he asked himself. Wolf had worked alone for twenty years, and you don't break a habit of that long standing in a few days. Wolf trusted no one and owed his liberty to that precaution; it was natural to continue that way no matter how much you liked a person.

Dave felt that Wolf did like him. He could sense it in the man's concern for him, in the way he had stuck with him and cared for him when he was helpless, in the way he spoke. He could see it in the warm light that sometimes came into Wolf's eyes, eyes that were usually hard and cold with suspicion. He treated Dave like a father would. And deep within him, taking firmer root every day, was a deep regard in Dave for this man they called El Lobo. He did not attempt to analyze the feeling; he supposed that one would naturally have a liking for a man who had risked his life for you. But despite this bond of friendship, Wolf shied away from taking Dave as a partner.

Well, he could wait. How long he would have to wait he did not know, but that waiting period would be shortened if he could prove to Wolf that he was capable, could remain cool under fire, could establish himself as dependable when the going was rough. This, he vowed, he would do. If Wolf did not assign him a job, he would find one for himself.

Hard work took the resentment out of him but did not weaken his determination to show the old master. He would take his time, plan carefully. He thought suddenly of Pat Downing. A wonderful girl, lovely, unspoiled, the kind of girl a man wants to marry. He knew in the same instant that he could not marry any woman. There is no room in the life of an outlaw for a wife. It would not be fair to her. He'd have all the excitement, and she nothing but worry and perhaps misery. Marriage was definitely out. Until after he'd made his pile, anyhow.

Although Wolf had told him to take Saturday off, he went back to work in the morning to make up for the time he had lost in crossing the basin the day before. When he had finished his dinner, he was tempted to ride over to the ranch and ask Pat to show him more of the country, but he put temptation behind him and rode to Santa Anita instead. Ranchers and cowboys had not yet come to town, and except for a few dozing Mexicans the street was empty. He tied his horse in front of the cantina and sat down on the bench outside the doorway.

A rider walked his horse into the far end of the street, halted, and for some seconds sat scrutinizing both sides of the road. He came slowly toward the cantina, his watchful eyes on Dave. He was a big man and as he drew near Dave saw a wide strip of court plaster running from the corner of his left eye to his chin. He did not come to the hitching rail, but turned off the street and rode along the far side of the cantina and out of Dave's sight.

Dave kept watching that corner, thinking the man would return. He sensed a presence at the other corner and turned his head. The man had circled the building and was standing there. He was rolling a cigarette, but Dave could see the dark eyes beneath the brim of the gray hat searching the buildings on the other side of the street. He twisted the end of the cigarette, scraped a match into flame with his thumbnail, lighted up. He turned then to look at Dave, nodded shortly, came over and sat down on the bench.

'Pretty quiet,' Dave said. 'Too early, for much business, I guess.'

'They call this place Santa Anita, don't they?'

'That's right.'

'Cattle country?'

'Mostly. Some mines in the hills.'

The man drew on the cigarette, exhaled slowly. 'You work around here?'

'In the basin.' Dave waved an arm in that direction.

'Cowhand?'

'I'm helping a man to build a house.'

'A rancher?'

The man, thought Dave, was asking an awful lot of questions. From his actions he could be a lawman, or he could be on the dodge.

'Well, he owns a ranch, but he's a cattle buyer. His name is Christopher Jones.'

Texas Jack felt a little thrill of satisfaction. He was getting his information easier than he had anticipated.

'He has a man run the ranch for him,' Dave

went on. 'His name is Will Downing. If you're looking for a job, he's the one to see.'

'Not right now. Picked up a little wad in a poker game and want to spend it first. Thanks for the tip, though.' He got up, flicked the cigarette into the street. 'Come in and have a drink.'

They went into the cantina. The only other occupant was Felipe Pacheco, who was dozing in a tilted chair. He opened one eye, squinted at them, then got up reluctantly and went behind the bar. Texas Jack bent a hard gaze on him. This was the test. If Wolf had told about the pistol-whipping, this man would know it and would betray his knowledge when he saw the strip of plaster. Pacheco gave his face only a casual glance.

They ordered tequila, and Texas Jack asked, 'Your boss comin' to town today?'

'Chris? No. He's in Briscoe. Won't be back until Monday.'

They raised their glasses and drank.

'What kind of feller is this Chris Jones?'

'Rough and tough and don't talk much. Not until you know him. Treats me fine. He can have my right arm any time he wants it.'

Dave ordered drinks.

'Let's set down and nurse this one,' suggested Texas Jack, and led the way to a table at the rear of the room. He set his drink on the table, went to the back door and tried it. It was locked, and he drew the bolt, opened the door and looked into the alley. Dave saw his horse standing beside the doorway. Jack closed the door but did not lock it. He came to the table and sat down facing the front entrance.

'Expecting somebody?' asked Dave.

'Not particular. I just don't aim to be crowded into no corners.' He touched the strip of court plaster gently. 'Got that from bein' hemmed in. Knife cut. Feel like a little two-handed poker?'

Dave said he did and Jack got a deck out of a pocket and they cut for the deal.

'I'm Dave Singleton.'

'Tom Smith, here.'

They played for small stakes for about an hour. Dave noticed that his companion kept his attention on the front entrance. He was no cowhand, decided Dave; his hands were too soft and he was too much on the alert. Tom Smith was not his real name any more than Christopher Jones was Wolf's. Like Wolf, he was probably on the dodge; if so, Dave wanted to know him better.

People were coming into town now; Dave could hear the rattle of wagon wheels and the slow thud of hoofs and the clumping of boots and the voices of men as they called greetings. Some cowboys came into the cantina, and after them a couple of miners.

'Let's call it off,' said Texas Jack. 'Gettin' too

noisy.'

He put the cards back into his pocket and they gathered up the small piles of coins before them.

'Got a place to bed down tonight?' asked Dave.

'I'm used to sleepin' on the ground.'

'Why don't you come out to the house and bunk with me?'

'I don't like sleepin' with a bunch of cowhands.'

'This ain't a bunkhouse. Chris and me live in a cabin near the north hills. Nobody within five miles of us.'

Texas Jack considered. 'Your boss might come back. Maybe he wouldn't like to find me there.'

'I told you he rode to Briscoe. That's forty miles, and his business will keep him there until Monday.'

Texas Jack wanted to learn all he could about El Lobo's hangout, and this seemed to be his chance. Here was a kid certainly not over twenty opening the door for him. He nodded.

'All right, I'll take you up on that, Davey. We'll get a bottle of tequila and make a day of it. I'll pull out in the mornin'.'

They went to the bar and bought the bottle of tequila. Dave wanted to pay for it, but Jack insisted it was his treat.

'Told you I'd made a little pile and wanted to

get rid of it. My hoss is out back. Get yours and join me there.'

He went out the back door and Dave went out the front. Dave got on his horse and rode around the cantina, and they set off along the alley. They cut across the basin, and when they had topped a rise, Dave pointed out the speck which was the cabin.

'There it is. The ranch is over there.'

Jack drew rein when they were still some distance from the cabin. 'You scout on ahead, Dave. If your boss has come back, give me the highball and I'll vamoose.'

'He's not back. If he was, his horse would be in the corral or somewhere in sight.'

'I'd rather you made sure first.'

Dave nodded and rode ahead. Tom Smith sure acted like a man on the dodge, and if he was he might be willing to take on a partner for a job or two. If so, Dave would have the chance he wanted to show Wolf what he could do.

Wolf, of course, was not at the cabin, and Dave waved Jack to come on. They stripped their horses and put them into the corral and went on inside. Jack looked critically about him.

'Nice place, Davey. Clean. Don't look much like bachelor's quarters.'

'Pat Downing keeps it clean for us. She's the manager's granddaughter. Make yourself at home, Tom. It's quiet here. We can go on with that poker game if you want to.'

They played, sipping drinks as they did so. Neither had any intention of getting drunk, and in any event there was not enough tequila to make them anything more than talkative. Texas Jack did not lose his caution; from time to time he would go to the door and take a long look.

'Tom,' said Dave after one of these surveys, 'you sure are uneasy.'

'Just careful, Davey.'

Dave leaned across the table. 'You don't have to play foxy with me. You're on the dodge, ain't you?'

Jack gathered up his cards, arranged them. 'What makes you think that?'

'The way you acted back there at Santa Anita, looking the town over before you rode in, tying your horse behind the cantina and unlocking the door so you could get to him easy, the way you watched everybody that came in. Ever hear of a man named Ed Grant?'

'Seems like I have. Sheriff or marshal or somethin', ain't he?'

'Sheriff with a roving disposition. Don't stick to his own territory when he's after a man. I just wondered if he's after you.'

Texas Jack did not answer. He was studying his cards intently.

'I know he's looking for me,' went on Dave a bit proudly. 'I held up a blackjack dealer and Ed Grant happened to be in the saloon. I didn't know him then. I just managed to get away.' He got up, pulled out his shirt and raised it so as to show the bandaged side. 'Gave me a little souvenir to remember him by.'

Jack stared at the bandage. 'Well, I'll be damned!'

'So,' said Dave, stuffing in his shirt, 'you don't have to worry about me.' He sat down again.

This, Jack decided, would explain why the boy was hiding out with Wolf. Just the same, he was puzzled. El Lobo had always worked alone, and if at this late date he had decided to take a partner, it certainly would not be a green kid like this. Green, yes; or he would not have admitted that Ed Grant was after him, nor would he have answered all those questions back at Santa Anita until he knew more about his companion. Tom Smith could be a law officer, who was pretending to be on the dodge.

All Texas Jack offered in reply to Dave's assurance was: 'I'll open for a dime.'

Dave understood that the subject was closed for the moment, but he felt that he had made a beginning.

Texas Jack slept in Wolf's bunk that night. He slept fully clothed and with his gun on the chair beside him. He saddled up after breakfast the next morning.

'I'll be in Santa Anita next Saturday,' Dave said. 'You and me hit it off pretty good. Fact is,

I kind of thought we might go into business together.'

'What kind of business?'

'The same kind that got me this.' He touched the bandaged side.

Texas Jack looked down at him. To Jack, the wound was no badge of merit, and the kid was too eager and green to have his offer taken seriously, but through this boy he could keep tabs on Wolf. And perhaps Dave Singleton could be fitted somewhere into his plans.

'I'll think it over,' he promised.

'You'll keep in touch?'

'You'll be hearin' from me. So long.'

He wheeled his horse and rode off toward Santa Anita.

Dave walked around to the front of the cabin and looked after him. He was still looking when his attention was caught by a rider coming from the direction of the ranch and discovered it was Pat. He awaited her arrival with a mixture of pleasure and reluctance. As much as he liked Pat, he must not let her affect his plans.

She rode up and saluted him gaily. 'Hi, Dave! That wasn't Uncle Chris who just rode away. Did you have company?'

'Just a feller who wanted to know if that was Santa Anita. Chris went to Briscoe to see about milled lumber and hardware. We're building a new house.'

'What in the world for?'

‘Oh—’ He made a vague gesture. ‘Just to keep busy, I guess.’

‘I rode over to ask both of you to dinner. You’ll come, won’t you?’

He wanted to beg off, but could find no excuse. ‘That’s nice of you. Wait until I throw on a saddle and I’ll be with you.’

It would be the last time, he told himself. He must become no further involved with Pat Downing. Better to break off now rather than later. He’d have work on the house to blame for refusing to ride during the week, and on Saturdays he’d go to Santa Anita. On Sundays he’d have to find something to take him away from the cabin.

There could be no room in his life for a woman from now on out...

CHAPTER NINE

Wolf rode at a fast trail gait, for he wanted to get to Jupiter that night. He would look over Mike Maloney’s place as soon as he got there and would pull the job the next night, Saturday, when there would be a maximum of cash on hand. His horse would have all day Saturday to rest.

He had never before been bothered with scruples about lying, but he found the lie he had told David distasteful. This annoyed him, as had his failure to kill Texas Jack when he had the chance. The sudden acquisition of a grown son had completely changed his way of living and thinking. While his own robberies and killings disturbed him not a bit, the thought of Dave as a thief and killer was frightening and abhorrent. He fathomed the boy's intense affection for him and his desire to emulate him, and now for the first time he was riding on a job from necessity rather than choice. He wanted to keep the boy with him, and to do that he must keep Dave busy. He could do this by building the house, and he must have money to build it.

He ate in the saddle and stopped only to rest his horse and let it drink. He made Jupiter before midnight, stripped the tired horse and picketed him in a grassy hollow and walked the mile to Mike Maloney's saloon and gambling hall.

There were no people on the dark street, and when he entered Mike's place he saw only a scattering of regulars at the bar and five playing poker. Tomorrow night the place would be filled to overflowing.

He paused briefly at the poker table to watch the play, then bellied up at the far end of the bar. Here he could look through an open doorway into a small room which Mike used as an office. There was a roll-top desk with a lighted lamp on it, and beside the desk was the safe. Wolf knew there was a door in that office opening on the staircase which led upward to Mike's quarters.

Mike, redhaired and muscular, came to where Wolf stood and looked him over while awaiting his order. Wolf called for whiskey. Mike served him, said, 'You've been in here before, haven't you?'

'A couple of times.'

'Knew I'd seen you before. Got a good memory for faces. Wasn't sure, though. Just can't place you. Live around here, do you?'

'No. Just passing through.'

Wolf drank, stood for a moment fiddling with the empty glass, then turned away. He mustn't seem too much in a hurry. He paused again at the poker table, watched two or three hands, then sauntered out the door to the street. He walked to his camp in the hollow, rolled in his blankets and went to sleep.

He did not go to town the next day. No use taking his chances. Mike Maloney had a good memory for faces, although Wolf had shaved off his mustache. He had no business in Jupiter anyway, having seen the night before that the layout was the same as he remembered it.

He spent the time loafing and planning out his procedure for Saturday night in considerable detail . . .

* * *

Since he did not go to town he missed seeing the two men who rode into Jupiter just before noon. One was a United States marshal named Zach Short and the other was Sheriff Ed Grant.

After the escape of Wolf and Dave from the ravine, Ed and his posse had conducted a thorough search along the desert's west fringe. Not finding trace of the fugitives, Ed had dismissed the posse and had continued the search alone. He had bumped into Marshal Short, and since the Federal Government also wanted Wolf for mail robbery, he enlisted Short's aid. They had ridden southward almost to Santa Anita, then had decided to try their luck in the north, stopping at every town and broadcasting a description of Wolf, which did not include the now famous mustache.

They rode into Jupiter tired, hungry and dirty, and since the town had a hotel, they decided to put up here for the night, scouting the town that afternoon and evening.

They washed up, ate dinner, and went along the street questioning storekeepers and saloonmen and citizens. They learned nothing until they questioned Mike Maloney, then they struck pay dirt.

'Sure, I seen him! He was in here last night. I remembered his face. Got a good memory for faces, I have. But him not wearin' a mustache, I couldn't place him. He's your El Lobo, all right.'

'You wouldn't know if he's in town now?'

'Said he was ridin' through. It was late, though. After midnight. He might have bedded down in a hayloft or somethin'.'

'We'll look,' said Grant. 'Keep your mouth shut.'

They made their search. They did it methodically, Ed taking the street and Zach the alley. They kept abreast, and when Ed went in the front of a store or other building, Zach covered the rear. When they finished the buildings on the street, they took those in the alley, examining every shed and stable and barn. They did this on both sides of the street and found no trace of El Lobo or his blaze-faced bay with the white stockings.

'He ain't in town,' decided Ed. 'He could hide somewhere, but he sure couldn't hide that hoss of his.'

'We could make up a posse and search the surrounding country.'

Ed thought this over, shook his head. 'He'd spot us, and he's as slick as a fox. No, I got me an idea. His stopping in at Mike's place last night looks to me like he was sizing the joint up. If he aims to rob the place, he'll do it tonight. It won't cost us anything to lay a little trap. I nearly got him that way once before. Let's go back to Mike's and figure out a little surprise for Mr. Wolf.'

*   *   *

Wolf made his move at midnight. He saddled up and rode across country to the stable behind Mike's place. He tied his horse in back of this, circled the saloon and crossed the street to a grocery store which was now closed. He sat down on the steps to wait. Except for the glow from lighted saloons and the few business places still open, it was utterly dark.

It would be three o'clock or later when Mike would chase out the last hangers-on and bar the doors, but he must go in at least an hour earlier. He thought of Dave and found himself wishing that he didn't have to do the job at all. He had led a lonely life so long that being in the company of the boy gave him the keenest enjoyment he had ever known.

It would be heaven if he could quit this life and settle down in the basin in peace and contentment, with Dave's and Pat's kids playing and shouting and climbing over him. Yes, sir, that would be heaven; the nearest to a real heaven that he'd ever get.

He shook his head, his eyes bleak. There was no peace and contentment for him anywhere. Always must he keep running and hiding. Perhaps he'd never see the basin and Dave again. In this risky game, you never knew how the dice would fall. He'd been lucky so far, but who can say how long Lady Luck will stay with a man?

He had to go through with it. He had to have money to build that house and there would be no beef sales until fall. The ranch was already involved with mortgage loans; most of the fall beef money was earmarked for the bank, so he couldn't borrow any more from that source. And except for the Downings and Dave he had no friends. His lips twisted; Dave certainly had a distorted idea of the joys of an outlaw's life. He muttered, 'God keep him from it!' without realizing that this was the first prayer he had said since he was a child.

He sat there until the stars told him it was about two o'clock, then got up and strode across the street. The loud voices of men, the thump of glass on the bar and the click of the roulette wheel spilled out of the place. He glanced over the doors, saw nobody he knew, and went inside.

The bar was filled and all the games running. The smoke was thick and the big whale-oil lamps glowed like twin moons in a cloudy sky. He went down the side wall, moving slowly, pausing at each gaming table for a few moments, scanning faces without appearing to do so. Mike was too busy at the bar to test his memory for faces, but there was a broad-shouldered man at the end of the bar nearest the doorway who turned his head to scan everyone who entered. Wolf was sure that he had not been noticed by this person, who might have been a banker, a gambler, or a rancher in his going-to-town clothes. The name Zach Short would have meant nothing to Wolf.

He moved between a faro layout and the poker table and discreetly slipped past a group of talking men to the door of the broom closet. He put his back to it, found the knob with his fingers and turned it. The door opened outward, swinging toward the front of the saloon. He waited until the moment came, then opened it quietly, backed into the closet and bumped into a yielding body which gave a grunt of surprise.

He wheeled and found his face six inches from that of Ed Grant!

Consternation held them both for a fraction of a second. The sheriff was squeezed back against the brooms and mop handles, Wolf was just within the doorway. Their bodies touched.

Wolf leaped backwards. He slammed the door against the lunging sheriff, forcing him back again. There was no lock. The back door was fifteen feet away and would be in Grant's range of vision the instant he opened the door. He could drill Wolf before he could get through to the alley.

These thoughts came to Wolf's mind in one instantaneous flash. He turned and ran to the door of Mike's office. He yanked it open, leaped inside. He heard a shot at the front of the bar and splinters flew. He closed the door and shot the bolt.

Outside there was sudden bedlam—men shouting questions, the pound of booted feet, the booming voice of Ed Grant. He heard the knob rattle and then the door shuddered as Grant hurled himself against it. Ed was shouting, 'Zach! Watch the outside! Watch the horses!'

There was no light in the office, but Wolf knew what he must do. He stumbled into Mike's swivel chair, snatched it up, smashed it against a window, breaking glass and wood. He dropped the chair, turned to his right, moved forward until his outstretched hands found the wall. He followed the wall until his fingers found the door opening on the staircase. He opened this and went up a step, then closed the door behind him.

He climbed the steps two at a time. What he was going to do he did not yet know; all he knew was that if he had gone through the window men would be outside waiting for him.

There was a bracket lamp burning in the upstairs hall, and he ducked into the first doorway he saw. It was Mike's bedroom. Downstairs they were trying to batter down the door with an axe or sledge.

The bracket lamp threw a faint light into the bedroom, and he saw in the ceiling the outline of a scuttle leading to the attic. It was above a bureau and there was a chair beside the bureau. He got on the chair, stepped to a cleared space on the bureau. He lifted the scuttle cover and pulled himself into the attic. He put the cover back into place, stood up and bumped his head on an overhead rafter. He squatted on his heels and thumbed a match into flame. There should be another scuttle leading to the roof.

There was. It was fastened with hooks that were rusty, but he got them loose, pushed aside the cover and got to the flat roof. From below, came the sound of a splintered door and the rush of feet into the office. Would the broken window mislead them? He could only hope.

He lay down and put his head through the scuttle opening. He heard boots thump on the stairs and clump into the bedroom. He heard somebody say, 'He ain't in here. Must have got out that window.' The boots went out and clumped into another room.

Wolf lay down on his belly, slithered to the edge of the roof and looked into the alley. The place swarmed with men, some of them carrying lanterns. The lanterns moved like fireflies, this way and that. He heard a voice from behind the stable, 'Here's his horse!' It was the voice of Ed Grant.

A vague shape of a man came around the corner of the stable leading a horse.

Ed Grant's voice said, 'I want every horse in

town corralled and brought to the street outside the saloon. I want them held there with a dozen men guarding them. Zach, take men and circle on the town. Keep them moving and don't let anyone get past you.'

Wolf grinned. It was a feral grin, the tight drawing in of lips that showed fangs. Ed Grant was doing things with his usual efficiency. He had Wolf's horse, knew that Wolf was still somewhere in town. His first step was to see that Wolf did not get out; the second, to search every spot that would afford a hiding place, including the roofs.

Wolf made a circuit on hands and knees. Nowhere could he find anything which would give him a footing on the way down; just a straight drop of twenty-five or thirty feet. The space between the saloon and the adjoining buildings was too wide for even a kangaroo to jump. It looked hopeless.

But now Wolf was in his element. For twenty years he had avoided traps or escaped from them. There was no longer any fear, any doubt. He would get away and he would get away before daylight. He had to.

He crouched on his heels in the middle of the roof and considered. All available men were taking part in the gathering of horses, riding circle, or ferreting out hiding places in the dark alleys. If he could get out of the building he could join the searchers and go unrecognized in the darkness. After all, the only one who knew him was Ed Grant, and it was dark enough so his features would not be recognized.

He got up, went to the scuttle hole and lowered himself into the attic. He stood listening for sounds from below, heard none. He raised the cover of the scuttle leading into Mike's bedroom, listened some more.

He heard sounds from the ground floor and the sounds told him that Mike was closing the window shutters. He got down, went out into the dimly lighted hall and looked down the stairs. The door at the bottom stood open. He heard the grating of a wooden bar as it was pushed into its sockets. Mike was locking up and that meant that he was probably alone.

Wolf turned the wick of the lamp even lower. He crouched against the wall in the deep shadow cast by the bottom of the lamp, drew his gun and waited.

There was a light in the office now, and by it he saw Mike come through the doorway to the saloon. He carried a bulging canvas bag: the night's take. Mike stepped gingerly over the splintered remains of the door, shaking his head and clucking at the damage. There came a slam and a clink and Wolf knew he had closed and fastened the shutters on the broken window. And then Wolf heard the pleasant clink of coins as the bag was emptied on the desk.

Wolf went down the stairs cautiously,

reached the bottom and looked around the door frame. Mike was sitting at the desk, his back to Wolf, sorting the coins and putting them in stacks.

It was ridiculously easy. Wolf snapped his gun into line, crossed the floor quietly. Mike sensed his approach when he was three feet away and swung around in the swivel chair. He looked squarely into the muzzle of Wolf's .45.

'Put it back in the bag,' said Wolf quietly. 'And thanks for closing the shutters.'

Mike's eyes flamed and his red hair seemed to bristle. He was thinking of resisting, but Wolf's hard face advised against such foolishness. He turned slowly back to the desk, started putting stacks of coins into the canvas bag. Wolf moved around the desk and tried the safe. It was locked and there was no time to fool with it. The last stack of coins fell into the sack.

Wolf said, 'Put your arms over the back of the chair.'

Maloney did so.

There was no rope available, so Wolf whipped off Mike's belt and with it bound his arms in such a way that he could not get free of the chair or reach the belt buckle with his fingers. He took a bandanna from his pocket, knotted it in the middle and put the knot into Mike's mouth. He tied the ends behind the man's head and picked up the bag. It was pleasantly heavy.

He went into the darkened saloon, and looked through a front window at a street full of horses and a circle of men guarding them. One horse stood alone at the hitching rail and he guessed it was Ed Grant's. He unbarred the door, opened it, and pushed part way through the swinging half-doors. Two of the guards had reined around and he knew they were watching him suspiciously.

He called to the vacant interior behind him, 'All right, Mike, I'll hunt him up and report back to you.'

He pulled the door shut and pushed out to the street. The two had walked their horses over to the plank sidewalk.

'Where's the sheriff?' Wolf said boldly.

'Searchin' houses up the street. Who are you?'

Wolf held up the bag. 'Mike wants me to give him this. Figures it'll be safer with Grant while that Lobo feller's around. Mind if I borrow this horse? Mine's somewhere in the bunch. I'll be right back.'

He got on the sheriff's horse as though confident that they would make no objection, which he wasn't sure about at all. They didn't, and he rode past them and up the street. When he had gone a hundred yards or so he turned into a passageway that led to the alley, and then out into the open country at the edge of town. Here the starlight was fairly bright and he hadn't gone a hundred feet when he saw a horseman. The man had pulled up and faced him.

'Halt there! You can't get through.'

'I don't want to. Ed Grant sent me out to help ride circle. Haven't located that Lobo feller, and Ed's afraid he'll slip past you.'

'Ain't nobody gettin' past us, especially if he's on foot. Fall in about fifty yards behind me. I got a feelin' that somebody's goin' to collect the bounty on a wolf pelt tonight.'

'Hope it's me. That five thousand bucks will buy a lot of liquor.'

'Yeah, it will. Invite me to the party.'

He rode on, and Wolf waited a few moments, then fell in behind him. The man disappeared in a dry wash which crossed his path, emerged on its far bank. Wolf rode into it and did not emerge. He followed the bed of the wash until he was a mile from Jupiter, then headed for home.

The coins in the canvas bag clinked merrily . . .

CHAPTER TEN

Wolf rode straight westward, then cut south, and dawn found him a dozen miles from Jupiter and going strong. Around noon he came to a water hole and saw several horses grazing near it. He took the sheriff's rope from the saddle and roped one of them.

He tied the free end of the rope about the neck of the sheriff's roan so that he could control both animals while he switched rigs. He mounted the fresh horse and rode on, leading the sheriff's horse. He had to get rid of the roan and he dared not turn it loose for somebody to find.

He came to a range of hills and climbed into them, and finally found what he was looking for, a brush-choked, steep ravine. He halted on its brink and shot the roan through the head, then unfastened the rope and rolled the dead animal into the ravine. After that he made better time.

He made camp by a spring and picketed his horse so that it could graze. He tightened the rawhide thong he was using for a belt and had a smoke for his dinner. He set out again as darkness was falling, and now he headed eastward, coming finally to the road between Jupiter and Briscoe. He followed this, riding all night, and entered Briscoe early on Monday morning.

He put the horse in the livery corral with instructions to cool out the animal and give it a good grain feed, then went into a restaurant and ate a big breakfast. At the lumber yard he ordered the milled lumber they would need, and at a hardware store purchased nails and some tools. He had the purchase put into a burlap sack and lashed it to the saddle. Before noon he was headed for Santa Anita. It was close to ten that night when he sighted the lighted window of his cabin.

Dave came out to meet him.

'Howdy, son,' said Wolf as he swung to the ground. 'How'd things go?'

'All right.'

They started to strip the gear from the horse.

'This isn't your horse,' said Dave.

'Mine lamed himself and I had to swap.'

Dave put the horse into the corral, threw some hay over the fence. Wolf hung the saddle in the shed and took off the bundle of tools. They went into the house together. Wolf took the tools out of the sack and displayed them on the table.

'You get them at Briscoe?' asked Dave.

'Yes.'

Wolf looked at the boy. Dave's face was impassive and his voice without inflection.

'What's the matter, son? I told you I was going to Briscoe.'

'I know you did. It just happened that I took the glasses into the hills with me. I watched you and saw you turn off the road to Jupiter.'

'So you don't believe I bought these things at Briscoe?'

Dave shrugged.

Wolf fished in a pocket and produced slips for the hardware and the lumber. He handed them to Dave and Dave read them. A frown of puzzlement came into his face.

'I tell you,' he said slowly, 'I saw you on the Jupiter road, headed north. I rode across the basin to make sure.'

'I had my reason for taking that road,' said Wolf quietly, 'and I don't have to tell you what it was. Now I'm hungry and I'm going to eat.'

'I'll get it,' Dave offered quickly. 'You sit down and rest. I'm sorry, Wolf. I got no right to question you; it was just that I thought—'

'Forget it,' Wolf cut in roughly, and sat down in the rawhide chair and got out his pipe.

Dave was cheerful once more. He fanned the fire into life, rattled pots and pans. He asked questions. What kind of a town was Briscoe? Did Wolf have any trouble getting lumber? Where did the horse go lame? Where did he get the one he was riding?

Wolf answered some of the questions, dodged others by asking some himself.

'Take Saturday off like I told you?'

'Worked in the morning to make up for the time I wasted riding across the basin. Went to Santa Anita in the afternoon. Had dinner with the Downings on Sunday. The best meal I've had since Mother died.'

'Stay for supper?'

'No. I came home early. It's like I told you;

Pat and me are just friends. It ain't like I was courting her.'

Wolf told himself that people do not fall in love overnight; it would take time to turn this friendship into something stronger.

He ate, and Dave sat across the table from him and sipped a cup of coffee. They talked about the house and became enthusiastic, and, his suspicions gone, Dave was smiling and happy again.

They resumed their work of cutting timber the next day. Dave was lighthearted, and Wolf was as near to that state as he would ever be. At noon they ate a lunch they had fetched up with them, sitting side by side on a log. Once, when Dave made some particularly witty quip, Wolf laughed and put an arm over the boy's shoulders and hugged him. They were very happy together; like father and son . . .

★ ★ ★

In a cluster of rocks about a mile from where they were working, was Texas Jack. For most of the morning he had lain on his belly watching them through a pair of glasses. The more he watched, the more puzzled he became.

He knew El Lobo to be a man sufficient unto himself, with no friends and suspicious of everyone; but with this Dave Singleton he seemed another man. Jack saw the hug Wolf gave the boy and was more bewildered than ever. Wolf's every action betrayed his intense liking for Dave.

Jack lay there scowling, wondering how he could turn Wolf in and collect the bounty. He had first thought of using Dave, but Dave was evidently too much attached to the outlaw to betray him. He had said Wolf could have his right arm any time he wanted it.

He had thought briefly of killing Wolf and to hell with the reward, but his greedy soul had rebelled against this except as a last resort. Besides, killing Wolf would not be easy. Right now Wolf was within easy range of his glasses but not of his rifle. By choosing his route he could work right into the trees where they were cutting, but he would have to get very close in order to have a clear shot, and the slightest crackle of brush would alarm the wily Wolf and then it would be curtains for Texas Jack. And there would be Dave to consider, too. No, this was not the time or the place; the sign wasn't right.

He watched until they had dragged their logs to the site of the house and knocked off for supper, then went to his horse and rode to his camp. He was still trying to figure a means of turning Wolf over to Ed Grant and collecting the reward without risking his own neck...

The week passed with Wolf and Dave working together and enjoying it. They got out enough logs to make a start on the house, and went to shaping and fitting with adze and saw. Dave, regretting his suspicion of Wolf, worked cheerfully and steadily, for the time being subduing the urge to make a quick stake by unlawful means.

The matter of the saddle did not come up during the week. Wolf kept it in the shed with his blanket hung over it, and when they had ridden into the hills and back it was so covered with tools and equipment that Dave did not notice the slight difference in color and trappings.

Texas Jack still watched from the hills, although he had changed location when they had moved down into the basin. He watched them in their occasional recreation periods when they horsed around, wrestling, jumping, shooting at targets. Sometimes they just sat and talked; but everything they did bespoke an affection on both sides that was firmly rooted.

It seemed that Wolf had suddenly gone in for companionship, and he had gone full out. He and the boy acted like brothers, or a particularly devoted father and son. Jack's eyes narrowed. Could be. Wolf had undoubtedly known women who had admired him for his exploits; he could have gotten married years ago, at the start of his outlaw career, and had this son . . .

It was then that Texas Jack got the idea. If

Dave Singleton was Wolf's son, the best way of hurting him was through that son. Put a bullet into a man's head or hang him at the end of a rope and his misery is over in a matter of seconds; hurt someone he loves and his suffering lingers.

* * *

All that week Dave did not visit the Downings or mention them. He seemed content to play cards with Wolf and turn in early. On Friday, Pat rode over to see them. She invited them to Sunday dinner, and Wolf accepted at once. Dave said nothing, and he did not go outside with Pat when she left. This troubled Wolf.

'You and Pat have a falling out?'

'No.'

'We won't work tomorrow, you know.'

Dave nodded. 'Think I'll ride in to Santa Anita. Want to go along?'

'No. Nothing there to see or do. Ask Pat to ride in with you.'

'You just said there's nothing to see or do. I'll go alone.'

He rode to town the next morning, going early so as not to see Pat if she came over. He knew he would enjoy riding with her, but having firmly decided that a break between them was for the best, it was a pleasure he must deny himself. Also he hoped to meet Texas Jack in Santa Anita.

He stopped at the store to buy some tobacco, then rode to the end of the street and back again. He dismounted in front of the cantina and sat down on the bench. He rested his back against the wall, pulled his hat down over his eyes and dozed. The bench jiggled when somebody sat down beside him, and he opened his eyes and saw the man he knew as Tom Smith.

'Tom! I hoped I'd run into you.'

'Said I'd keep in touch, didn't I? Your boss in town?'

'No. Said there was nothing to see or do.'

'How's the house comin' along?'

'Fine. It's fun working on it. Chris is a swell man to work for.'

'Treats you like a son, huh?'

'Yes, I guess he does. I wouldn't know. My father was killed in the war before I was born.'

Texas Jack nodded. If Dave was really Wolf's son, it would be only natural for the mother to tell the boy something like this when he was old enough to ask about his father.

'You thought any more about the proposition I spoke of?' asked Dave.

'I'm still thinkin'. Feel like a drink?'

Dave said he did and they went into the cantina. Felipe Pacheco was alone; he served them tequila and they carried it to the table they had occupied the week before. Once more

Texas Jack made sure that the rear door was unbolted. They had just started a game of poker when they heard the thud of hoofs and the rattle of wheels. Jack stiffened and put down his cards.

'Must be the stage,' said Dave. 'Pat Downing told me there was one every Saturday. Changes horses here and lays over at Briscoe tonight.'

'Take a look.'

Dave went to the doorway and saw the stage pull up at the corral beside Mendoza's store. The driver called a greeting to Juan and tossed down a slim pouch. He tossed the lines to a Mexican stock tender, climbed down and came across the street towards the cantina.

Dave returned to the table.

'Two passengers,' he reported. 'Both women.'

The driver came in, said, 'Howdy, Felipe. How about some ice-cold beer?'

'Only tequila.'

'As if I didn't know it! All right, pour me a snort.' He drank the liquor, pushed the glass over for a refill. 'Seen anything of El Lobo?'

'You are joke. El Lobo never comes to Santa Anita.'

'You wouldn't know him if he did. He ain't wearin' that mustache of his no more.'

'W'at he do now?'

'Just about turned Jupiter upside down. Last Saturday night.'

Both Texas Jack and Dave were listening. Dave had turned in his chair.

'W'at he do?'

'Came into Mike Maloney's place late Friday night, had one drink and went out again. Mike didn't recognize him without his mustache. On Saturday, Ed Grant and Marshal Zach Short rode into town to spread the word that El Lobo had shed his whiskers. When they told him, Mike remembered the man of the night before and knew he was Lobo. Ed Grant made a wild guess that El Lobo aimed to hold up the joint that night and hid in a broom closet. And all of a sudden that closet door opened and there, b'God, was El Lobo! Starin' Ed right in the face, belly to belly.'

He drank the tequila, wiped his mustache.

'An' den?'

'All hell broke loose. El Lobo jumped back and slammed the door and ducked into Mike's office. Locked the door and smashed a window. Everybody thought he'd got out that window, but it turned out that he ran upstairs and got through a scuttle to the roof.'

He continued his account of Wolf's risky but profitable activities early that Sunday morning. 'Now Ed Grant's out his favorite hoss,' the driver finished, 'and Mike's minus a couple thousand dollars . . . Well, see you next week. And, say! Keep your eyes open for El Lobo. They've added another twenty-five hundred to that reward, makin' him worth seventy-five hundred to the feller that fetches him in, on the hoof, or head-down across a saddle—either way!'

He went out, and Dave turned to look at Tom Smith. His eyes were shining. The fact that Wolf had lied to him was forgotten in the thrill of the exploit.

'What a man!' said Dave. 'It takes real guts and plenty of brains to pull a deal like that!'

Tom Smith's face was hard and cold. 'Ever see this El Lobo?'

'No; but wouldn't I like to meet him! God, what a man!'

'I'd like to meet up with him, too. Seventy-five hundred bucks is a lot of *dinero*, Davey. Over thirty-five hundred for each of us. Sure you don't know him?'

'If I did, I wouldn't turn him in for a million. He got it the hard way, let him enjoy it.' He leaned forward in his eagerness. 'Tom, why can't we pull something like that? Something big! Something that'll make a whole town sit up and take notice! You and me! How about it?'

Texas Jack studied him. This boy must know that the man he worked for was El Lobo. He had covered for Wolf by declaring that Wolf had gone to Briscoe the week before; he was covering for him now by pretending he did not know him.

Or was it possible that he had attached

himself to Wolf without knowing his identity as El Lobo? Certainly he had not accompanied Wolf on the Jupiter job. He thought it over for a moment. If Wolf was the boy's father, perhaps he would not want his son to know the truth about him, would want him to think he was honest and upright. That would explain Wolf's telling the boy he was going to Briscoe instead of Jupiter.

'Maybe we will pull somethin' big,' he told Dave. 'Yeah, it might be a good idea. I'll look around a bit. Come in next Saturday and I'll let you know if I've anything lined up that looks good.'

CHAPTER ELEVEN

They parted right after that. Texas Jack said he wanted to think over a project he had in mind, and Dave was anxious to get back to the cabin and tell Wolf what he had heard.

He was seething with excitement as he raced homeward. El Lobo had done it again! Thrillingly, dramatically he had accomplished his purpose when the whole deck was stacked against him.

Wolf was seated on the bench outside the cabin door when Dave rode up, jerked his horse to a standstill and hit the ground. He dropped the rein, strode to the bench, put his hands on Wolf's shoulders and shook him.

'You old son-of-a-gun, you did it again!' he cried, his eyes shining. 'If the last name is Wolf, the first should be Fox!'

'What're you talking about?'

'The Jupiter holdup. The stage driver told about it in Santa Anita. Last Saturday, maybe you did go to Briscoe, but you went to Jupiter first. Both Ed Grant and a U.S. marshal were laying for you, but you outfoxed them and got off with Ed's horse and two thousand in cash!' He threw himself on the bench beside Wolf. 'Tell me about it. Tell me everything.'

'It was nothing to brag about,' said Wolf gruffly.

'Nothing to brag about! Just listen to the man!' And he recounted briefly the highlights of Wolf's adventure as he had heard it. 'And then, he says it was nothing to brag about!'

'Yes, that's what I said. With the luck I had, anybody could have done it. Damn it, Dave, I told you I'm no hero; I told you I always take the coward's way. Why don't you believe me!'

'Why should I believe anything you say? You told me you were going to Briscoe; you went to Jupiter instead.'

'I did go to Briscoe. I bought lumber and hardware and tools there.'

'Sure—after you'd finished at Jupiter. But I don't mind your lying to me, Wolf, and bucking a whole town ain't my idea of being a coward, not by a long shot!'

Wolf made an angry, impatient gesture. 'There wasn't one bit of courage in anything I did. You can't call it courage when you do the only thing you can do. I acted like a scared rat by instinct, and I had a lot of luck. Was it courage that made me jump away from Ed Grant and slam the closet door in his face? Did it take courage to duck through the first door I came to? I tell you I went into that office like any frightened rat would dive into the nearest hole. Was it brave of me to smash that window and then run upstairs and get on the roof? I just did the only thing I could do to save my miserable hide, and I was scared sick while I did it.'

'Yeah? How about going downstairs again and sticking up Maloney? How about walking out and stealing the sheriff's horse right under their guns?'

'Damn it! I tell you I had no choice. I knew if I stayed on the roof I'd be nailed and the only way down was the way I came up. I knew they'd searched Maloney's place, and I heard him shutting doors and shutters and knew they'd gone outside. Maloney and me were alone in the building, nobody could see us from outside, and I had a gun. I stuck it in his ribs and tied him up. The money was there and I took it. What's so damned brave about that?'

'And you're trying to tell me it didn't take nerve to walk out into the street and take the sheriff's horse?'

'That's just what I'm trying to tell you. I couldn't stay on the roof, I couldn't stay in the building, and I couldn't stay in the town. I had to get out. I had no choice. Nobody knew me by sight except Ed Grant, and even if they had it was too dark to make out my features. I walked out into the street and called something back to Maloney like, "I'll see you later," or something like that. I don't remember. I was too scared. I told the guards Maloney had sent me to find Ed Grant. His horse was the only one handy that was saddled, and I said I'd fetch it right back and got on and rode away. When somebody stopped me, I said I was looking for Ed and thought he was with the boys riding circle. There was nothing to it. Once riding circle I slipped away the first chance I got.'

Dave took a deep breath.

'Well, you can call it luck or instinct or anything else you want to; I still say it took nerve and plenty of it. Not only nerve, but quick thinking. Quick and—and brilliant. Wolf, I'd have given an arm to be with you. Why, oh, why can't you trust me enough to take me along!'

'If I had, neither of us would be talking about it now. I had only myself to think of; if I had to think of you, too—' He broke it off with a gesture.

'If I had been along you'd have played it differently. I could have scouted the place first. If I had found Ed Grant in that closet, he might have grabbed me, but all he had against me was that tinhorn's holdup. I would have got a few days in jail and you wouldn't have had to fight a whole town.'

'Maybe; maybe not. Suppose you lost your head and tried to shoot it out with Ed Grant? That would have been just too bad for you.'

Dave gave him a long look. 'You don't give me much credit for brains, do you?'

'It's not that, believe me. I told you what a stinkin' damn mistake I made when I got into this business. I don't want you to do the same. God, boy! Can't you see that? I know what's ahead of you and I like you well enough not to want you to make a mess of your life as I have mine. Take my offer; buy the ranch, marry Pat and earn your stake honestly.'

'I'll buy the ranch some day, but it'll be with cash on the barrel head.' He looked off toward the Downing house and saw a rider heading for the cabin. He got up, went to his horse. 'Be seeing you,' he said, and started towards the corral, leading the animal.

He was gone before Wolf noticed the rider and recognized Pat. It was nearly half an hour before she pulled up at the cabin.

'Was that Dave I saw riding up into the

hills?' she asked.

'The hills? Why, I don't know, Pat. I thought he was putting his horse in the corral.'

'It was Dave. Why did he ride away?'

'I reckon he didn't see you coming. I didn't myself, until after he'd gone.'

She got slowly from her horse and came over and sat down beside him.

'Uncle Chris, what have I done to make him angry? He hasn't been over all week.'

'Well, for one thing we've been quite busy. We're building a new house, you know.'

She nodded. 'He told me. But this is Saturday and you don't work on Saturday, do you?'

'No. Dave rode to Santa Anita but didn't stay long.' He slanted a look at her. 'Kind of like him, don't you?'

'Yes.'

'Well, I happen to know he likes you.'

Her face brightened. 'Does he really?'

'He sure does. Don't say much about it, but I can tell.'

She turned cheerful at once. 'You're both coming over to dinner tomorrow?'

'We'll be there.'

'I'll fix something extra special.' She jumped up. 'Good-by, Uncle Chris. Come over early. And thanks a lot!'

She ran to her horse and leaped to the saddle. She turned her head to scan the hills in the hope of seeing Dave but did not. She reined away, waved a hand at Wolf, and started for home.

Wolf looked after her, his face twisted into a scowl. Dave had seen her coming and had ducked out to avoid meeting her. He had gone to Santa Anita early for the same reason. He remembered the boy insisting that they were just friends; evidently he was determined to keep it that way.

He asked himself why and found an answer. Dave was bent on getting a big stake the wrong way, and hearing of Wolf's exploits at Jupiter had merely strengthened his determination. He was gentleman enough not to want to hurt Pat by making her the sweetheart or wife of an outlaw, so he was trying to break off their affair before it became serious. And there was nothing Wolf could do about it.

Damn it! Why couldn't the boy listen? Why did he persist in believing that Wolf was trying to discourage him merely because the outlaw was afraid to take a chance with him as a partner?

He was living in a dream; the dream of wealth acquired easily and quickly in a land where lawless men flourish. All he could think of was lifting a Wells-Fargo box with twenty thousand in it; holding up a bank with a vault crammed with banknotes; robbing a gambling hall where thousands of dollars passed over the tables in one night. What he did not know was that so often the Wells-Fargo box contained only hundreds in cash, or only valuables like jewelry or non-negotiable securities; that the bank vault was generally locked; that the thousands that passed over the gambling tables generally revealed themselves to be only a fraction of that amount. And the personal risk he dismissed with the blithe confidence of youth. Disaster always came to others, never to him.

And the gall in Wolf's potion was that everything the outlaw did simply confirmed those beliefs. Now, after Jupiter, the boy was fired with a new enthusiasm for crime.

Dave was not gone long. Evidently he had been watching Pat from the hills and had returned as soon as she reached the ranch house. He put up his horse, came around the cabin and sat beside Wolf.

'Pat saw you duck out,' Wolf told him bluntly. 'She thinks you are trying to keep out of her way.'

'Does she?'

'I do, too. It just ain't natural for a young feller to run away from a handsome girl like Pat Downing.'

'I know. It's just that we've been riding around together a lot and I don't want her to get the idea that I'm in love with her.'

'Are you?'

Dave was silent for a moment. 'It don't

matter whether I am or not. You know what I aim to do. I want a wad of dough to wave under Grandpap's nose and I want it before he kicks off. If you won't take me with you, sooner or later I'll strike out on my own. If anything happens to me, I don't want a woman grieving over me. Or me over her.'

'Still got that crazy idea in your head, huh?'

'Yes. And when I see what you've done, I don't think it's so crazy.'

Wolf gave it up; they just talked in circles. He went to the site of the new house and hacked angrily at logs, and presently Dave joined him and they worked together. It wasn't long before they were laughing and joking again. Neither could remain angry with the other very long.

They rode over to the Downing house the next morning, and since Pat was busy in the kitchen, Dave sat with the two older men and talked cows and horses. He did not see Pat until she called them to dinner.

It was the first time he had seen her in other than range clothes, and the sight quickened the blood in his veins and made his heart beat harder. Before, she had seemed more like a younger tomboy sister; now she had been transformed into a lovely and desirable young woman. She wore a becoming print dress and her light brown hair was gathered in a cluster of soft curls tied with a scarlet ribbon. He tried not to look at her too often or too long.

She donned a long apron over the dress and he helped her clear the table and wash dishes. He wanted to get away but could find no excuse for leaving without being downright rude. She suggested a ride, and he had to agree. She changed into riding clothes and they set out. He thought that perhaps seeing her in levis and flannel shirt again would break the spell, but it did not.

They rode up into the hills, she chatting gaily, he enjoying the chatter with a little bell in the back of his brain ringing a warning. They came to a spring among a grove of trees and got off to drink the fresh, cool water. They lay down on their stomachs at the edge of the pool and drank from cupped hands, then looked at each other, chins dripping, and laughed.

And then he put his arms about her and kissed her.

It lasted but a moment, then he put her from him and got to his feet. He was angry with himself, because he had yielded to an impulse that he could not resist. Pat got up slowly, turned to look at him. Her eyes were soft and her lips slightly parted. He knew she expected him to kiss her again.

He said shortly, 'We'd better be going,' and strode to his horse.

'But we've just got here! And it's such a lovely place, Davey.'

'Don't call me that!' he said sharply, and saw the smile go out of her eyes. He added quickly, 'I'm sorry, Pat. I didn't mean to be so rough. But that kiss—it was an accident. Forget it.'

She came over and stood very close to him. 'I don't want to forget it. I want to remember it. Always.'

'I said to forget it. It didn't mean a thing. Come on; let's go.'

He turned and swung up into the saddle, for the first time not helping her to mount. She stood for a short space looking up at him, and he did not look at her because he knew her eyes were clouded and perplexed and very near to crying.

Slowly she lifted herself into the saddle and they turned back.

He forced the pace, making it impossible for them to talk. She rode for a short distance with drooping head, then straightened in the saddle and put her chin in the air. He felt miserable.

He kept telling himself that this was best for her sake. She must not suffer ever because of him. But he was sick at heart and never so near to forgetting his purpose. Perhaps he might have forgotten had he not thought of Wolf. He had told Wolf that he would show that he was worthy of being the outlaw's partner and that he must do.

They reached the ranch without once speaking, and Pat slipped off her horse and went right into the house. Dave off-saddled her horse and put it into the corral, then went around the house and sat on the edge of the gallery until Wolf said he guessed it was about time they were going.

Wolf studied him occasionally as they rode homeward, but he did not ask questions. Perhaps he was afraid of the answers he would get.

They worked together all that week. At first Dave was silent and glum, but as the days passed his spirits rose and once more they were father and son. Wolf told himself that there had been a lovers' spat and that in time they would make it up. It was comforting, even though he did not believe himself. He was even more tender that week, humoring the boy, cheering him with amusing prattle, every once in a while putting his arm across Dave's shoulders in that gesture we reserve for ones we love.

Gradually a sense of relief came over Dave. He had made the break, and Pat, her pride cruelly hurt, would not look him up again. He was free of all encumbrances. He began looking forward to the meeting with Tom Smith on the following Saturday . . .

★ ★ ★

Texas Jack kept watching them, noticing the signs of growing affection between them. It galled him to know that El Lobo, cold and hard and lethal, had permitted himself to become so firmly attached to this boy. Jack was now convinced that Wolf was really Dave's father, and was equally sure that the boy was unaware of the relationship. Certainly if Dave was in danger, Wolf would turn the world upside down to get to him.

This thought gave birth to an idea, and he pondered over it all the rest of the week. Wolf would not walk into any of the ordinary traps, but use Dave for bait and he would forget his caution.

He began to plan, and when all the details were fixed in his mind he broke camp, got on his horse and rode to the Acme mine...

CHAPTER TWELVE

The Acme mine was located in the Thunderheads, some forty miles south of Jupiter. It was a large and productive mine with its own stamping mills and smelters. On an average of once a month the gold ingots were transported under heavy guard to the railhead at Jupiter and shipped to the mint.

Only once had this shipment been successfully held up, and that was in the early days when the amount shipped was comparatively small and the guards numbered but two. The successful robber was El Lobo. With a rifle at an extraordinarily long range, he had killed one guard and wounded the other, chased the man who led the pack mule carrying the shipment and forced him to surrender the precious load.

He crossed two states, avoiding pursuit with his usual skill, and had settled down as a prospector, melting the ingots into nuggets or filing them into dust, and had lived in luxury for two years. It was the Acme which had offered the original reward of five thousand dollars for the capture or killing of El Lobo, and his name was still anathema to them.

Texas Jack reached the mine on Friday afternoon and entered the shack which was used as an office. This was divided into two rooms, one used by Harry Thompson, the super, the other by a little bald-headed bookkeeper. The latter, wearing a shade over his eyes and paper cuffs on his sleeves, was perched on a stool before a high desk. When Jack came in, he looked up inquiringly and said, 'Yes?'

'I want to see the super.'

The man jerked his head towards an open doorway. 'In there.'

Jack went through the doorway and saw another man seated at another desk. He was also small, hard-faced and cold-eyed.

'You the super?'

'That's right. Who are you?'

Jack closed the door, sat down in a chair beside the desk. 'Name's Tom Smith.'

'I'm Harry Thompson. If you're looking for a job, we're carrying all the help we need at present.'

'I've already got a job. Holdin' up your next shipment. Interested?'

'Naturally. I don't suppose you came here to tell me how you're going to do it?'

'That's what I came for, providin' we can make a deal.'

The super leaned back in his swivel chair, fixed Jack with a cold stare.

'Deal, huh? What kind of deal?'

'A deal that'll hand El Lobo over to you on a gold platter. You remember him, I reckon?'

'Too well. Now tell me how you expect to hand him over to us.'

'He aims to hold up your next shipment. Me and another guy are supposed to help him. I can fix it so that you can nail him and put him out of business for good.'

Thompson studied the stranger, wondering where the joker was hidden. He saw a man wearing fairly decent range clothing, an almost new gray Stetson hat, and a gun hung low on his thigh. He saw a smooth-shaven face with a soiled wide strip of court plaster running from the left eye to the corner of the mouth, black hair that needed cutting, shifty dark eyes and a slightly crooked nose.

'We could change the route and the date of the shipment,' he suggested.

'Sure you could. But how would that help you to get El Lobo? He'd still be around to take you. If you want to nail him, you better play my way.'

'Keep talking.'

'Like I told you, I'm in on the deal. Even with El Lobo bossin' the job, I don't like it. He's been crowdin' his luck lately and it can't last. Ed Grant nearly got him at Jupiter, a week ago last Saturday. I don't want to play on his team. If I remember right it was your outfit that put the five thousand on his head, dead or alive.'

'Right. Dead or alive, we're not particular.'

'You can have him either way, but if I steer him to you I want that reward.'

'Why don't you take your information to the law? We've authorized them to pay the reward. And there's been another twenty-five hundred added that you could collect.'

'Happens,' said Jack drily, 'that me and the law ain't on speakin' terms. I might make a deal to swap El Lobo's hide for mine, but if so, they ain't goin' to pay me no seven thousand five hundred. You can bet a stack of blues on that.'

'I see. Just how do you propose to turn him over to us?'

'If you go along with me, I'll show you how it

can't miss. But first I want somethin' in writin' bindin' the Acme to pay me that reward and protectin' me by keepin' it quiet.'

Thompson thought it over. Then he said: 'Sounds reasonable enough. If we do it ourselves, none of the guards can claim the reward, because they're being paid for guarding that gold.'

He drew a sheet of company letterhead and wrote out a brief agreement to the effect that if El Lobo were captured or killed as a result of information furnished by Tom Smith, as identified by signature, the company would pay said Tom Smith the sum of five thousand dollars and do it without harmful publicity. He signed the statement, handed the paper to Texas Jack, who signed it as Tom Smith after reading it, then folded it and put it into his pocket.

He drew his chair nearer to the desk, lowered his voice. 'Now here's how El Lobo aims to work it.' He took a paper from his pocket, spread it on the desk. It was a rough sketch map of the route usually taken. He pointed with a stubby forefinger. 'Now here the trail runs for a mile or so through a ravine which narrows down right here. El Lobo aims to mine both banks with blastin' powder. One of us will be on each side ready to light the fuses when your party comes in sight. The other will be on the bank, far enough away to be behind you when she blows. When the fuses are lighted, the two that lit them will run along the banks a safe distance away. When she explodes, the banks will cave in, blockin' your way. Got it?'

Thompson nodded. 'Go on.'

'You can guess the rest. We'll have you cold, covered from the banks above you. The three of us can pick off your guards one at a time if we have to. If they ain't completely loco, we won't have to.'

Thompson smiled thinly. 'El Lobo hasn't done a good research job. We're quite aware of that bottleneck and its possibilities. When we come to it, guards are sent along the tops of both banks. Your men would be spotted, and—disposed of.'

'I told you that the Wolf's slippin'! He hadn't counted on that. But you might get him and you might not. He's mighty slippery. And you still want him, don't you?'

'So much that I'll go along with you all the way.'

'Keno! Now this is how it'll have to be played. March your guards right along that ravine bed and into the trap. Tell 'em not to put up a fight, just throw down their guns and push their hands in the air like they're ordered to.

'We'll come down and tie 'em up good and proper. Wolf and the other feller will take the pack mule in tow and light out. I'm to hang back as rear guard and cover the trail, just in case. They'll head for that old lumber camp down here.' He pointed to a spot marked X on the sketch map. 'They'll shoot the mule and divide the ingots into three parts for easier carryin'. By the time they got this done, I'll be with 'em. We'll each take our third and split, goin' different directions. That's the way it's supposed to be.

'Now what me an' you will do is this: The minute they get out of sight, I'll come back and free the guards. You'll have another bunch followin' them a little distance back. They'll come up on the run and the whole bunch will circle around to that old lumberjack's cabin where we're to meet. Since they'll be leadin' the pack mule, we oughta get there ahead of them. We'll keep out of sight, and when they go into the cabin we'll surround it, and—there they are. Starve 'em out or burn 'em out, get back the gold and give Wolf and his pal their needin's. How do you like it?'

He settled back in the chair, a complacent smile on his face. Thompson studied the map, checking the plan over for flaws and finding none. He nodded. 'Looks good so far. One thing sure, it's no job for a lone hand; the stuff's too heavy for one man to tote and make the speed he's got to have.'

Texas Jack nodded, grinning widely. 'It won't take me thirty seconds to cut the guards loose, and if the second bunch is close enough we can be after them within a minute. Hell, no matter what they try, we'll nail 'em.'

Thompson turned the swivel chair back to the desk. 'Now let's figure out just how we'll do this.'

It took an hour to plan the whole thing, and try to foresee and answer every possible objection. During that hour the bookkeeper sat in on the conference. The guards would not be told of the scheme until just before starting out with the shipment. The time was set a week from the next day, Saturday.

Jack rode away feeling rather proud of himself. Dave Singleton would fall for this hide, hock and hair. Stealing a shipment from the Acme gold mine! He'd have every right to be thrilled, Jack thought cynically.

Dave was about the same height as Wolf, wore the same kind of clothes. Put a mask over his face and the guards would take it for granted that he actually was Wolf. The fact that only two of them would appear at the holdup would arouse no suspicion; they would assume that the third was covering the operation from the top of the ravine. Now all Jack had to do was to get Wolf at that lumberjack cabin when Dave reached it with the stolen shipment, and already Jack had figured out how to do this. They would be trapped together . . .

Back at the mine, the bookkeeper said to Thompson, 'You're not really going to send the gold along, are you?'

'Not by a jugful. This man Tom Smith would take the gold teeth out of his mother's mouth—if she had any. The whole talk about El Lobo might have been cooked up by him so he could get his paws on the gold. Hunt up or buy a few pigs of lead and iron. We'll make an amalgam and have it cast into ingots. Gild them.'

* * *

Dave and Wolf worked on the house all week. The logs went up, tier on tier, and the structure began to take on form. On Thursday a freight wagon arrived from Briscoe with the milled lumber, roofing tiles, the rest of the hardware, and also paint and cement. They stacked the lumber carefully so that it would not warp, built a stone sled and fetched stone for the fireplaces and chimney.

Dave had recovered his good spirits, although there were times when Wolf caught him gazing wistfully towards the distant ranch house. Pat did not visit them and Wolf refrained from mentioning her. They would get over it, he told himself; Pat loved Dave and Dave loved Pat. If only the boy would get this holdup stuff out of his head . . .

As Saturday approached Dave worked more feverishly than ever. Tom Smith had promised to find them a job, a big job, and he dreamed of it at night. He tried to imagine what it would be—a bank, a train, one of the larger gambling halls; maybe a Wells-Fargo stage station with a huge shipment of gold on hand.

One big strike was all he wanted, he told himself. Afterwards? He'd ride the outlaw trail with Wolf, and when Wolf decided to quit the game, he'd quit too. He'd buy the ranch, start courting Pat in earnest, marry her and settle down. Raising kids and cattle, Wolf had said. It sounded good to Dave. But first of all was the necessity for a stake.

He left for Santa Anita early on Saturday morning, Wolf once more declining to go along. He waited as patiently as he could on the bench outside the cantina, but it was nearly noon when Texas Jack joined him, having ridden since midnight. Dave got up and hurried to him.

'Where have you been? I thought you'd never get here.'

'Mostly ridin', lookin' after our business. I've got to dig up a fresh hoss somewhere. Your boss in town?'

'No. He's not coming in. You got something figured out?'

'I'll say I have! Come inside and I'll tell you about it.'

They went into the cantina. They bought drinks and carried them to the table at the back of the room. Dave gulped his drink, asked eagerly, 'Is it something big?'

Jack grinned across the table at him. 'Big enough even for you, Davey. A full shipment of pure gold in ingots. Fifteen, maybe twenty thousand dollars' worth.'

'My God!' gasped Dave.

'It'll be easy, too. Next Saturday afternoon. A shipment from the Acme mine, forty miles this side of Jupiter. As soon as I get me a fresh hoss we'll ride out there and look it over. Now this is how we'll do it . . .'

* * *

Ed Grant's dead horse was finally found by the rancher who had turned out the horse with a saddle sore. That animal was not with the other horses that had been turned out, and the rancher went in search of it. His search led him close to the Thunderheads, and wheeling buzzards in the sky caught his attention. They guided him to the ravine where Wolf had dumped the sheriff's horse and the rancher found a skeleton with a few patches of hide clinging to it. The color of the hair told him that this was not the horse he sought.

That weekend the rancher went to Jupiter for supplies and there he heard of the holdup of Mike Maloney's place by El Lobo. Ed Grant was searching the country around Jupiter, but rode into town that night. The rancher told him about the skeleton he had found, and the color of the patches of hide convinced Ed that the dead horse had been his.

Ed set out that same day, riding southward to the Thunderheads. He found the ravine within a mile of the Acme mine and looked at the remains. It was his horse, and the tracks, still visible, told him that Wolf had fled southward. How far south?

Ed was out of his jurisdiction and knew very little about this part of the country; but he did know that the road from Jupiter led to Briscoe. Ed rode on to Briscoe and went around the town asking questions, giving Wolf's description. Fairly tall, slim but strong and energetic, hard-faced and cold-eyed, sandy hair, no mustache, regular range clothing. He realized that the description would fit hundreds of men in and around Briscoe. He drew a blank.

'You won't find El Lobo anywhere near Briscoe,' the hardware man told him. 'You know he always gives a town a wide berth after he's done a job on it. And he came near to getting his some time back when he tried that holdup of the Citizens Bank. No, I'm right sure he's never been in town since.'

Towns around here? Nothing between Briscoe and Jupiter to the north but a little Mexican settlement called Santa Anita.

'Wouldn't have known it existed,' the man

told Ed Grant, 'if it hadn't been for a rancher named Christopher Jones who bought some hardware from me several weeks ago. He has a ranch in the basin this side of Santa Anita. I sent the stuff over to him in a freighter that was carrying milled lumber he'd ordered. Building himself a house. Ranch is four or five miles this side of Santa Anita.

'Hide-out for El Lobo? Well, I don't know. It's isolated, all right, but El Lobo's too foxy to hole up so near to Briscoe after that attempted holdup.'

The sheriff nodded and kept his own counsel. He decided that since he'd come this far, he'd spend some time looking around a little more to the south. Then, on his way back, he'd camp somewhere in that basin near Santa Anita and nose around a bit. You never can tell what you'll find in the most unexpected places . . .

CHAPTER THIRTEEN

In Santa Anita Texas Jack swapped horses with a Mexican and he set out for the lumber camp. Jack left first and Dave joined him a mile beyond the town. They reached the old cabin at the abandoned lumber camp around midnight. It had taken them eleven hours and their horses were almost exhausted.

'We'll need fresh horses next week, won't we?' asked Dave as they pulled the gear from their horses.

'I'll find a pair and stake 'em out near this cabin. We'll leave Santa Anita Friday evenin' around seven. That'll get us here around six in the mornin'. That'll give us six, seven hours to rest. I've timed them when they made other shipments and I know they figure on gettin' to the ranch where they bed down overnight just before dark. That will fetch them to the place I got picked for the holdup around three.

'Like I told you, we ride back here after the holdup and I'll get the fresh hosses. We divide the gold, load up and then get the hell out of here. Now we'll stake these critters out on grass, eat some grub I fetched along and get a little shut-eye. We'll talk it over tomorrow.'

They were up early and rode to the ravine where the holdup was to take place, Dave memorizing the route over which he was to return with the laden pack mule. They halted on the brink of the ravine and Jack pointed out what they must do.

'We mine both sides and one of us will be at each fuse. When the party gets within the right distance, I'll give the signal and we light up. We foller the banks down there to about where them rocks are. I'll be on this side, you on the other. Get it?'

'Yes.'

'She blows and plugs the ravine. The whole party will stop. We draw bead on 'em and tell 'em to throw down their guns. They'll do it.'

'Suppose they don't?'

'Then let 'em have it—it's no time to mess around. Any feller that don't shuck his gun, feed it to him. When we get 'em under control we go down and tie 'em up. You'll be wearin' your scarf over your face and I'll call you Lobo. You're about his build, and with a mask on they won't know the difference. It'll put the fear of God into 'em.

'Then, when we got 'em all tied up, you'll lead the pack mule down the ravine to a trail you can use gettin' to the top. Come on and I'll show you.'

They rode along the bank, stopping briefly at the spot they'd head for after lighting the fuses. Some distance beyond, Jack pointed out the trail which angled up the bank.

'When you get to the top, you'll head for the lumberjack's cabin. I'll hang back and cover the trail for you. At the cabin, you strip the mule and turn it loose. The ingots will be in two bundles, wrapped in burlap. Carry 'em inside the shack and wait for me. I'll pick up the fresh hosses and we'll load up and light out. That's all there is to it. How do you like it?'

'Sounds good. Where do we head for?'

'We split right at the cabin. Your best bet will be to strike east and then circle to the south and come into the hills behind the basin. What you do with your share of the gold is your business, but I reckon the best idea would be to bury it somewhere until the thing blows over.'

Burying the gold was a good idea, Dave reflected, but not until he had shown it to Wolf. He could make a complete explanation of his absence and win the hearty approval of the old master.

They rehearsed the holdup several times, until they considered themselves as nearly perfect as they could be.

'I won't go back to Santa Anita with you, for I got things to do at this end,' Jack said. 'I'll meet you at the cantina Friday evenin' as close to seven as you can make it.'

Dave rode away feeling grateful to Tom for giving him the opportunity to prove to Wolf that he was worthy of his salt. Just wait until he pulled up at the cabin with half a shipment of pure gold ingots lashed to his saddle!

It was after nine that night when he reached the cabin. He rode around to the corral and Wolf called to him and came into sight carrying a rifle. He had left the house at the sound of Dave's approach and had gone outside to wait until the visitor had been identified. He asked only one question.

'Had supper?'

'No. I'll fix something.'

Wolf strode into the cabin, and when Dave

came in he smelled frying steak and boiling coffee. Dave went out again and washed up and when he returned Wolf had the food on the table. Dave sat down and started to eat and Wolf lowered himself into the rawhide rocker and smoked.

'Not interested in where I was?' asked Dave between mouthfuls.

'You're a grown man. Where you go or what you do is no business of mine, as long as you show up for work on time. But when you didn't come home last night I figured maybe something had happened in Santa Anita. I rode into town this morning and asked Mendoza at the store if he'd seen you. He said you rode out of town around noon, headed north.'

'That's right. Nothing doing in Santa Anita and I figured to look around the country up north. Wound up by getting myself lost. So I camped out over night and finally found the stage road late this morning. I'd gone a lot farther than I thought.'

Wolf smoked in silence. Then: 'Yeah. Horse was pretty well used up.'

'Yes.'

'Funny what happens to a man who ain't a drunk. Now, the sun was nice and bright yesterday. Usual thing, sun rises in the east, sets in the west. Come a clear night, a man can see that the North Star is right in line with the end of the Big Dipper.'

'Meaning that you don't believe I was lost?'

'That's all right, son. I lied to you, and I reckon you got a right to lie to me. I was just afraid you'd run into some kind of trouble. Now that you're back, it's none of my business where you were.'

'I didn't pull any kind of job, if that'll make you feel better.'

'It does. You weren't cut out for an outlaw, son. Ain't nothing mean or ornery about you.'

Dave didn't answer; he turned in at once, for he was dog tired. He went over the plan in his mind before he fell asleep, re-enacting mentally every move he must make.

They went back to work on the house the next day. Time and again Dave went over his part in the holdup until he felt that he could carry it out in his sleep.

Friday came at last. That evening he must manage to be in Santa Anita by seven. Wolf made this easy for him. They finished supper by six, and Dave said, 'Think I'll ride to town. Need tobacco.'

'You can have some of mine; I got plenty.'

'Feel like riding, anyhow. And maybe I'll drop in on the Downings on my way back. Might even stay over, seeing that tomorrow's Saturday.'

'Good idea,' approved Wolf. 'I won't wait up for you.'

*   *   *

Dave reached Santa Anita before seven and found Tom Smith waiting for him in the cantina. He bought two drinks and carried them over to the table.

'Everything set?' he whispered tensely.

'All set. I got the ravine walls mined, I got the hosses staked out, and I got piggin' strings to tie up the guards. And grub in my saddlebags for a couple meals.'

'Tom, you sure are generous about this. You've supplied just about everything. Let me pay for some of the stuff.'

'Forget it, Davey. With all that gold comin' our way, what's a few bucks between friends?'

They drank their tequila, and it was time for Jack to make his final play, the play that would send El Lobo running into the trap.

'Davey, I been thinkin' over this thing all week. I don't see how it can miss, but there's one thing that would make it a lead-pipe cinch.'

'What's that?'

'Another man in the deal with us.'

'Yeah?'

'Look. When we hold 'em up, you and me got to go down into that ravine and tie 'em up. You can never tell what they'll do. If one got the chance to jump either of us there'd be a free-for-all and then we'd be two against a half dozen or more. Now if we had someone to stay at the top and cover us, nothin' like that could happen. See the point?'

Dave thought it over. 'I guess you're right, Tom.'

'I know I am. We both got to go down there, one to do the tyin' and the other to keep 'em under control while he's doin' it. I hate splittin' that gold three ways, but with another man helpin', then we'd know for sure things couldn't blow up in our faces.'

'Got anybody in mind, Tom?'

'No. I don't know anybody around here. I kinda thought you might get your boss, this Chris Jones feller, in on the deal. Think he'd come along?'

'I don't know,' said Dave slowly.

'Well, you know him; I don't. I just thought maybe he'd throw in with us, on account this is such a big job.'

Dave was staring at his glass, thinking. Wolf had consistently refused to take Dave with him—but what was the matter with Dave taking Wolf? The idea intrigued him. With Wolf along, Dave would have the chance to show him first-hand just what he could do. And with Wolf helping, there could be no doubt about their succeeding.

Texas Jack watched him closely. If Dave knew that the man he worked for was El Lobo, he'd be glad to have the outlaw with them; if he did not know, he might still count on Wolf's help because of their deep friendship. If Dave refused to ask Wolf, Jack had an alternate plan to get El Lobo to that lumber-camp cabin; but if Dave co-operated, it would be easy.

'Listen,' said Dave at last. 'I'm not sure about Chris. I *think* he'll go along. But if I go back and tell him and he refuses, then he might do something to queer the whole plan.'

'You can't go over and ask him,' said Jack, who had the thing figured out to the last detail. 'Take you two hours to ride over and fetch him. Tell you what: you write him a note puttin' it up to him and we'll send the note to him by a Mex kid. We'll give him the location of that lumber cabin and tell him to meet us there if he's interested. He can make it in twelve hours from his place, and that'll get him there by eight in the mornin'. If he don't show, then, we'll know he don't want no part of it.'

Dave nodded thoughtfully. 'I guess that's the best thing. I'll get some paper and write that note right now.'

Everything was working as Jack had planned. He took a dog-eared notebook from his pocket and tore out a page. He fished a pencil stub from another pocket and pushed both across the table to Dave.

'Write that note, Davey.'

Dave thought carefully, then wrote:

Dear Chris—I've found a job. It's a big one.

The boss says he can use another man. If you're interested meet me at the shack at the old lumber yard on the trail between the Acme mine and the Jupiter road . . .

Dave looked up. 'What time shall I say?'

'Not later than two o'clock on Saturday afternoon. That'll give him plenty of time and he won't have to use up his hoss.'

Dave added that information.

Jack said, 'Give me the note and I'll find a Mex kid to deliver it. You wait here for me.'

He took the note and went out, highly pleased with the way things were going. This Dave Singleton sure was still wet behind the ears. There was one slight alteration he must make in the note, so he crossed the street and went into the store. He put the note on a counter and carefully changed the word *two* to *three*. The holdup was scheduled for three o'clock, and Wolf must not reach that cabin before that time.

He now proceeded to make certain that this would not happen. He went down the street, saw a Mexican youth braiding a rawhide riata. He looked up at Jack and grinned.

'I want somebody to carry a message to Senor Jones, in the basin. You know him?'

'*Si*! At rodeo time I work for Senor Jones on the ranch where Senor Downing is manager for him.'

'I'll pay you a dollar if you take this note out to Jones; but I don't want it delivered until three o'clock in the morning. Savvy?'

'The senor will be in bed at that time.'

'I know that. You'll wake him up and call to him that you're leaving a note for him. Put it on the bench outside the door and ride away before he comes out. You must do this at exactly three o'clock. Then you say no word of this to anyone, or you'll never work for Jones again. Got it?'

The young man pocketed the note and the dollar. '*Si, senor. Claro.*' And the boy repeated the directions.

Jack returned to the cantina feeling sure that the man would keep his word. Everything depended upon his doing so, and Jack would have preferred a surer way of getting the word to Wolf but could think of none besides delivering it in person. That would be dangerous. And there wasn't time.

Wolf, starting about three in the morning, could not reach the lumberjack cabin before three in the afternoon, and to do so he must run his horse into the ground. Jack and Dave would leave the cabin at a few minutes after two, with Dave convinced that the man he had counted on had turned him down. Wolf would reach the shack on an exhausted horse just at the time of the holdup—the time having been agreed upon by the super at the mine. Everything had to work with clocklike precision, but a few minutes one way or the other would not matter. If Wolf arrived at the cabin before three, he'd wait for Dave; if he arrived a few minutes after three, he'd be within reach of the posse, and with a horse that was dead on its feet.

It all looked mighty good to Texas Jack.

CHAPTER FOURTEEN

Texas Jack and Dave left town as they had left it the week before, separately. When they met, they rode through the night, stopping only long enough to breathe their horses or to water them sparingly. They came to the trail which turned off the road and followed it, and reached the cabin at the deserted lumber camp at six o'clock. Their timing had been perfect.

They staked out their horses and bedded down in the cabin. Jack was snoring in a matter of minutes, but Dave did not sleep at once. He had a watch his mother had given him and he looked at it often by the light of a match. He wondered how soon Wolf would arrive.

They got up around noon and munched the rations Jack had fetched along.

'Chris should be here by now,' said Dave.

'If he's comin'. Got a couple hours yet. Reckon we ought to ride to the ravine and make sure everything's all right.'

They went out to saddle up, and Dave said, 'Wouldn't it be a good idea to get the fresh horses now?'

'They'll keep. I can pick 'em up on the way back, after we do the job.'

They rode the short distance to the ravine. The sun was high above them, the day was clear and warm and there was not a living creature in sight. They separated at the end of the ravine, Jack following the south bank, Dave the north.

They came to the place where the banks had been mined, and Dave found the length of fuse he was supposed to light. He marked its location in his mind, made sure that he had matches in his pocket. It was one forty-five when they returned to the shack. Wolf had not arrived.

'Reckon he ain't comin',' said Jack. 'Well, we can give him until a couple of minutes after two, then we'll pull it alone. We can do it, and that way there'll be more for each of us.'

Jack sat down, put his back to the wall and dozed. Dave walked about uneasily, staring often along the trail which led to the Jupiter road. He looked again at his watch.

'What time is it?' asked Jack.

'Five minutes of two.'

'We'll wait until five after.'

Two o'clock came, then five minutes after. Jack got up. 'Can't wait any longer. Let's get started.'

They saddled up and rode to the ravine. Once more they separated, taking opposite banks. They rode to the point where they would station themselves after lighting the fuses, tied their horses a short distance from the brink so that they would not be seen from below, then hunkered down by the fuses.

'We'll hear 'em before we see them,' said Jack, his voice carrying in the deep silence. 'After this, no talkin'. I'll wave my hand when it's time to light up.'

The silence bore down on them like a weight. Dave found himself sweating. He tried to relax, found it impossible.

Then Jack broke his rule of silence. He said sharply, 'Listen!'

From far up the ravine came the clink of iron shoe on rock, faint but unmistakable. Jack was holding something up for him to look at. It was a match.

Dave fumbled in his pocket, drew out two matches. He could hear the thud of hoofs, indistinct voices. He could not see them, but guessed there must be half a dozen or more of them. Jack waved his arm.

Dave scraped the match on a stone and put the flame to the split end of the fuse. He got up and ran for his station...

* * *

Wolf heard the hoofbeats while he slept, and their continuity impinged upon his brain and awakened him. Through the window he could see that it was still very dark, with no sign of dawn in the sky. He guessed it was close to three o'clock.

He knew after a few seconds of listening that there was but one rider and assumed at once that it was Dave. He lay with closed eyes but did not go back to sleep.

The hoofbeats slowed to a trot and then a walk. They ceased outside the cabin and he heard a hail that did not come from Dave.

'Senor Jones! I breeng the message for you. I put it on the bench.'

Wolf got up and hurried to the door, but before he could unbar it the messenger was racing away. He put down the bar, opened the door. He picked up the square of paper, went inside and barred the door, then lighted a lamp and read the note.

From Dave, and he said he had a job. Shack at the old lumber camp. If Wolf wanted it, he was to be there by three the next afternoon. Its significance reached him at once. Dave and at least one other had planned to hold up an Acme mine shipment, and they were inviting him to their party.

He swore, crushed the paper in a hand and tossed it into the cold fireplace. Beneath his dismay was fear for Dave. An attempt to hold up an Acme shipment was foolhardy; the gold was guarded by half a dozen armed men, and many precautions against surprise had been taken since the previous robbery.

He knew now where Dave had been the previous week; he had been scouting the route taken by the Acme when moving the gold. And his early leaving this time had its explanation, too: Dave had never intended spending the night at the Downing house; he had to get an early start in order to reach the log cabin in the lumber camp long before the holdup so that he could rest his horse. The poor kid did not know what he was up against. This certainly was not his own project; he knew nothing of the Acme mine and he spoke of 'the boss.' This must be somebody he had met at Santa Anita, one who knew of the shipment and had persuaded Dave that it could be successfully taken.

Wolf stood in the middle of the floor, thinking. If Dave wanted him in on the deal, why had he not sent the note before this? Surely he must have known that it would take a full twelve hours for Wolf to reach the lumber camp, and that he would arrive on a completely spent horse.

He got the note from the fireplace, smoothed it out and read it again. He had not been mistaken; he was to arrive there by three. He tossed the note into the fireplace again and dressed swiftly. He must stop Dave at any cost, stop him before he ran into utter disaster.

He ran to the corral, caught up his horse and saddled up. He pushed his rifle into the boot, and set out for Santa Anita at a headlong gallop.

It was close to four when he reached Santa Anita, and everything was dark. He pulled up at Pacheco's cantina, anchored his horse and ran to the lean-to built against it where Pacheco lived. He hammered on the door and called the man's name.

A voice from within said, '*Quienes*?'

'Chris Jones. Open up, Felipe; I must talk to you.'

A bar rattled and the door opened. Felipe Pacheco stuck his face out into the night. 'W'at you want, Senor Jones?'

'I have a man working for me—young feller about nineteen. Rode over here this evening around seven. Did you see him?'

'Yes, senor. He was in my cantina with another man he comes in with two, t'ree times before. They have one drink and the boy writes on paper and the other man takes the paper and goes out. Pretty soon he comes back and they leave, six, seven o'clock.'

'This other man—what did he look like?'

'Beeg man. Black hair, black eyes. He has the bandage on the left cheek. Comes from here to here.' He indicated with his finger.

'Thanks,' said Wolf, and ran to his horse.

Undoubtedly it was Texas Jack, and Texas Jack must be the one Dave referred to as 'the boss.' Jack had taken the note and left with it, which probably meant that he was the one who had found the messenger to deliver it. But Texas Jack knew that the Chris Jones to whom he had sent it was in reality El Lobo. Why had he permitted Dave to ask Wolf to join them? And if the note had been written between six and seven, then he must have arranged for the delay in delivering it. Wolf smelled a trick of some kind, but he had to go on. Dave was in a real jam, this time...

The sky brightened above the hill to the east and the sun came up. He kept riding while it climbed higher and higher, stopping once to rest his horse briefly. He knew the location of the camp. He saw by his watch that it was just a bit after noon and knew he would reach the shack on time.

He finally sighted the old log cabin through the thinning trees and halted his horse. The place appeared to be deserted but the feeling that this was a trap persisted; a trap baited by the one person in the past twenty years for whom he had known any affection.

He rode forward slowly and cautiously. If he was to meet Dave here at three o'clock, the boy should be at the cabin now; but there was no sign of life about the place. Cracks in the walls and roof admitted light and he saw through the doorless entrance that the building was empty.

Where was Dave?

And then came the distance-muted boom of an explosion. An instant later there came another. The sound came from the west. He did not know what had caused the explosions, but he was sure that Dave was somehow connected with them.

He spurred his horse toward the sounds...

* * *

Ed Grant sighted the buildings of a ranch near the foot of the southern range of hills. On the far side of the basin, opposite this ranch, was a cabin and a larger structure which was being built near it. The latter, he assumed, belonged to the rancher who had ordered lumber and hardware, a man named Christopher Jones.

He reached the Downing place and saw a young and pretty girl carrying a pail of milk from barn to house. She had stopped and was looking in his direction, and Ed touched his hat and waved a friendly hand. She set down the milk pail and waited for him. 'Morning, Miss,' he saluted her. 'Mind if I water my horse?'

'Good morning. There's a trough the other side of the barn. Help yourself.'

He thanked her and turned his horse toward the barn, and Pat Downing hurried to the house with the milk and came back to join him. They talked while the horse drank. She saw his badge pinned on his shirt pocket.

'I see you're a sheriff,' she said.

'Yes'm. Name's Ed Grant.'

'I'm Patricia Downing. I live here with my grandfather. He manages the ranch for Mr. Jones.'

'Jones, eh? The feller building the house the other side of the basin?'

She nodded.

'I heard he'd bought lumber in Briscoe. Used to know a Chris Jones years back, but lost track of him. What sort of looking feller is he?'

'Well, he's six feet tall, rather slim. Must be around forty-five or more. He doesn't mix with people much and seems awfully hard and cold. But really he isn't; not when you get to know him.'

'Live alone?'

'Yes. Or he did, until several weeks ago. He's a cattle buyer, and some stock he and a helper were driving were rustled and the helper was wounded. Uncle Chris brought the boy home with him and he's been there ever since. He's helping to build the house.'

Ed felt a sudden surge of exultation. The description of Christopher Jones agreed with that of El Lobo; the wounded boy he had fetched home with him could be the one Ed himself had winged.

'The boy bad hurt?'

'Not too bad, but he lost a lot of blood and was very weak for some time.'

'And they had their stock rustled, you said?'

She nodded.

The horse had finished drinking and was nibbling at the grass. Ed picked up the trailing rein. 'I'll ride over and talk to them. I'm looking for some cow thieves and they might be able to give me a lead. Don't know exactly when this happened?'

Pat did not, but she could give him the exact day they had arrived, and this fitted, too.

'Thank you very much, Miss Downing. I may be seeing you again.'

Ed set out to cross the basin. He rode briskly at first, but slowed down when he was within a mile of the cabin. He watched it carefully, and also the partially built house. He loosened the rifle in its sheath and made sure his Colt was hanging free.

He saw no sign of life about either building, and changed his course so that he could see behind the cabin, first from one side, then the other. He saw the pole corral, and its emptiness argued against the presence of anybody at the place. This did not cause him to relax his caution for you could take nothing for granted when dealing with El Lobo.

After twenty minutes of careful scouting and observation, Ed was satisfied that the cabin was empty, and he went inside. He moved about, examining each article he came to in the hope of finding some clue pointing to El Lobo. He came finally to the fireplace, crouched down and pawed among the ashes and ends of burned wood. He drew forth a crumpled sheet of paper, smoothed it out and read it. It was addressed to Chris and was signed Dave. It spoke of a job, a big job, and mentioned a cabin at a lumber camp off the Jupiter road. The roughly sketched map showed a trail leading to the cabin, which was marked with an X. Farther west was a capital A. Ed guessed the A stood for the Acme mine, near which he had found his dead horse.

The parts of the puzzle fell into place and Ed had it. He did not know too much about this part of the country, but he knew the Acme was one of the biggest gold producers in this part of the Territory, and 'the job' suggested a holdup of that gold.

Ed rode to Santa Anita, and on the way there he took off his badge and put it into a pocket. He went into Pacheco's cantina, had a drink. He was looking for an old friend named Chris Jones, but had been unable to find him at his house in the basin. Had Pacheco seen him?

'But yes, senor! This very morning. Very early; around four hours after midnight, he gets me out of bed and asks me if I had seen the boy who works for him. I told him that I had and that he was with a big man with a bandage on his face. He runs quick and jumps on horse and rides north like the wind.'

Ed nodded, smiling inwardly. He dropped a dollar on the bar, went out and got on his horse and sent it racing toward Jupiter.

CHAPTER FIFTEEN

Dave was crouched behind a rock when the explosions came. He saw dirt and stones catapult into the air and a rain of pebbles pelted him. While the air was still filled with debris from the second explosion, he pulled his scarf over his nose and ran to the lip of the ravine.

Below him, the party with the shipment had come to a halt. He saw horses dancing and riders huddling in their saddles against the rain of dirt and stones. He counted six of them, including the one who led the pack mule.

He looked across the ravine and saw Tom Smith standing on the brink with his rifle pointed at the group, and raised his own weapon to cover the man who led the pack mule.

Jack called, 'Everybody stand hitched! The man who makes a move gets it!'

Heads turned to look up at Jack and then swiveled quickly to Dave. All the men carried rifles but no attempt was made to use them.

'Throw the rifles away, all of you!'

They obeyed, and Jack ordered each in turn to draw his sixgun and drop it. Again they did as he directed. Dave marveled at the ease of it.

'Lobo,' Jack called across the ravine, 'go down there and take care of them. I'll cover you.'

Dave urged his horse over the brink, leaned back in the saddle as the animal leaped and slid to the bottom. He halted the horse on a mound where he could dominate them and covered them while Jack came down. When Jack had reached the ravine bed, Dave shoved his rifle into its sheath and drew his Colt. He dismounted and ran to the man at the head of the column, spoke gruffly as he imagined Wolf would have. 'Get down.'

The man dismounted and Dave made him lie on the ground, face down. Dave took two of the pigging strings Jack had given him, tied the man's hands securely behind him and lashed his ankles together.

He went along the line doing the same to all of them. Not one opened his mouth to protest, not one offered any kind of resistance. In five minutes flat, all six were lying on their faces, bound hand and foot.

'Get that pack mule, Lobo, and clear out,' ordered Jack.

Dave picked up the lead rope, led the mule to where his horse stood, and mounted up. They had agreed that Jack would stampede the horses when he was in the clear.

Dave set off at a trot, pulling the pack mule after him. He reached the trail which slanted up the side of the ravine and put the animals to the climb. At the top, he headed for the trail which led to the old cabin.

He realized now that he had been under a terrific strain the whole time. Sweat was cold on his forehead and every nerve and muscle was taut. But now it was over. Not a shot had been fired, the party from the mine were helpless at the bottom of the ravine, and at the end of the lead rope he had tied to his saddle horn was a shipment of gold ingots!

He laughed excitedly. They had done it! All that remained was the getaway and that should be just as easy. Unload at the shack, wait for Tom Smith to fetch the fresh horses, divide the loot, then back to the basin, to an astonished and admiring Wolf!

He tried to figure in his head just how much his share of the gold was worth. Seven thousand? Maybe more. Not enough to buy Wolf's spread, but enough to make quite a wad of banknotes to wave under Grandpap's nose.

The mule kept dragging back on the rope and the going was rough, so he pulled down to a walk. It was about a mile from the ravine to the shack and he had covered nearly half the distance. The first of the trees in the stretch of woods where the lumber camp was located were just ahead of him; mostly small, second-growth stuff. He reached it and halted, intending to bring the mule abreast of him. And then he heard the crackle of brush ahead and had a glimpse of a horseman among the trees.

His blood seemed to freeze and for a moment he could do nothing; then he jerked out his Colt, raised it to cover the vague form of the rider.

'*Dave*!'

He lowered the sixgun, relief showing on his face.

'Wolf! Man, where've you been?'

He spurred forward to meet the rider. He went on excitedly, 'Wolf, we did it! Fifty pounds of gold ingots from the Acme mine! Now maybe you'll say that I'm good enough to take along!'

Wolf's face was haggard and his eyes burned. 'Where's Texas Jack?'

'Texas Jack? Never heard of him. Feller that I'm with is named Tom Smith.'

'Got a strip of court plaster on his left cheek?'

'Yes. Knife wound.'

'Knife wound, hell! He's Texas Jack and that was put there by the front sight of my gun. Where is he?'

'Covering the back trail. Wolf, you're wrong. His name is Tom Smith. Ride along with me; I got to get to the shack and unload so we can split the gold as soon as he comes up.'

He sent his horse ahead and Wolf fell in beside him. 'What held you up?' asked Dave. 'I sent you that note last night before seven.'

'You sent it? Or Texas Jack?'

'I tell you his name is Tom Smith. He sent it; said he knew a Mexican boy who would deliver it. And he told me he saw the boy start for the basin before he left him.'

'He lied. The note was delivered to me at three this morning and it gave me till three this afternoon to get to this cabin.'

'Three? You mean two, don't you?'

'I said three.'

'But I wrote two! I can't be wrong about that, it was too important. The holdup was set for three.'

'It said three. I can read. Texas Jack changed the time and told the boy not to deliver it until three this morning.'

'But what would he do that for?'

'Because he didn't want me to get here until the holdup was over. I tell you I pistol-whipped him and he's thirsty for my blood and the reward. He knew you were going to send for me? Suggested it?'

'Well, yes. But he didn't know you're El Lobo. He thinks you're a rancher named Chris Jones.'

'He knows I'm El Lobo. He recognized me in Mendoza's store and heard the old man call me

Senor Jones. That's when I pistol-whipped him, and he planned this whole deal to suck me in. I tell you this is a trap!' He reached out and seized Dave's rein, pulling the horse to a halt. 'Son, turn loose that pack mule and let's get out of here.'

'No! Wolf, you're wrong; dead wrong. How can it be a trap? Would he give up eight, ten thousand dollars just to pay you back?'

'He made a deal with the Acme people. They're so anxious to get me that they'll pay five thousand for me, dead or alive. He can't collect through the law, for he's wanted, too. But he can collect from the mine, and no questions asked.'

'But why would the Acme people risk losing this gold shipment?'

'That's what I'm wondering.' He got off his horse. 'Let's take a look at it.'

'We haven't got time. I've got to get to that cabin.'

'We're going to take time.'

He seized the lead rope, walked along it to the pack mule. Dave sat his saddle looking back at him. Wolf took out his knife, opened it. The ingots were in two bundles, as Jack had said they would be, one on either side of the pack saddle. Wolf ripped the burlap covering with the knife blade and Dave saw the yellow sheen of one of the bars.

'Satisfied?' he said, half angrily. 'Now come

on and let's get to that cabin.'

Wolf scraped the ingot with the point of the blade, flashed a quick look at Dave. 'Come here and take a look.'

Dave, suddenly apprehensive, slipped from the saddle and ran back to where Wolf stood. Wolf made a cutting motion with the knife. The metal beneath the gilt was a silvery gray.

'There's your gold,' said Wolf tightly. 'You're towing a hundred pounds of lead and iron. It's been gilded, that's all!'

Dave was staring at the metal. He took Wolf's knife and scraped the gilt off another bar. He felt suddenly as though he had swallowed the whole fifty pounds and it had settled at the bottom of his stomach.

Wolf said quietly, 'I reckon you see the play now. Texas Jack makes a deal with the Acme to draw me into a fake holdup, if they'll pay him the reward direct. He uses you to suck me in. He changed the time in the note from two o'clock to three and tells the boy not to deliver it until three in the morning. That way he's sure I won't get here before the holdup. Right?'

Dave nodded. It was all very clear—now. Tom Smith—or Texas Jack—knew the exact time the shipment would reach the ravine, and had also seen to it that the guards would not put up a fight. It had been easy; too easy.

He said dully, 'Yes. It had to be that way. Now he's supposed to be watching the back trail, but instead he'll cut those guards loose and head for the shack. He figures you'll be waiting for me there, and—'

He turned and strode to his horse, and Wolf leaped after him and caught him by an arm. 'What are you going to do?'

'I'm going back there and get him!'

'No, you're not. He has those guards with him now; maybe a second party which was following the first. They'll shoot you down on sight.'

'I don't care as long as I get him. He used me to get you into this mess and he's not going to live to brag about it.'

'I'll say amen to that, but we won't do it your way. You'll never get close to him. Get on your horse and we'll ride back to the cabin. That's an order, son.'

They mounted and set out. 'What are we going to do?' Dave asked.

'The best thing for you to do is head right for the basin and leave Texas Jack to me.'

'You can count that out. Where you go, I go.'

Wolf glared at him, saw that he was determined and could not be moved. His hard eyes suddenly warmed. He said softly, 'Okay, son. It's you and me to the end of the line.'

They reached the old log cabin and dismounted. 'What do you do next, according to the plan?' Wolf wanted to know.

'Strip the mule and carry the gold inside.

Then Tom—I mean Texas Jack—comes up with the fresh horses, we split the gold and go our own ways.'

'All right. We'll strip the mule and carry the bundles into the shack.'

As they did this, Wolf looked at him. The boy seemed older, more mature. He had learned a lot in the last half hour, and probably the most important thing he had learned was that there is no honor among thieves. He had learned to hate. And the man he hated represented everything Wolf wanted him to hate.

'What do you think Jack is going to do from here on?' asked Wolf.

'I think he went back and turned those guards loose. He didn't stampede the horses. They'll circle to this shack, leave their horses at a distance, and surround it if they think we're inside.'

'That's what we want them to do, so they must think we're inside. That means we must leave the mule and our horses where they are. Then we pull away and wait for them. They'll need every man they got, so they won't leave a guard with the horses. We must spot Texas Jack, and between us we'll get him. We make a break for their horses, take two of them and stampede the rest. Sound all right?'

'Yes. The trouble will be spotting Texas Jack.'

'Right. Let's go.'

They went out of the shack, moved along the trail toward the ravine until they reached the last of the trees where Dave and Wolf had met.

'They won't follow the trail,' said Wolf. 'They'll circle in one direction or the other so as to come to the shack from the sides or the back. When we see which way they're coming in, we can beat them to it and find places where we can watch them.'

They did not have long to wait. Within minutes they saw twelve horsemen ride into view where the ravine levelled out.

'There were only six of them in the ravine,' said Dave.

'Had another party following. Let's go.'

They ran back along the trail and followed it to a point a hundred yards beyond the cabin. They cut to the south then, going through the underbrush to a clump of alders.

'They're coming in from this direction,' Wolf said. 'Texas Jack is leading them. He's the one we must watch.'

They waited. They heard no sound of hoofbeats and knew the party had dismounted and were leading their horses. By standing up they could see through a gap in the trees, and presently the party came in sight, leading their horses and moving slowly and quietly. They did not speak, but each tied his horse to a tree, then followed Texas Jack in single file, walking like

Indians. A little distance past the place where they watched, the file halted and Jack made a motion with his arm, pointing toward the shack. The last man in line started off in that direction, and the rest moved on.

Wolf and Dave slipped from their cover and circled wide. They passed the man who had been posted at a safe distance. They reached the place where they thought Jack would post himself and found cover.

'Here he comes!' whispered Dave tensely.

They saw Texas Jack edging through the brush, treading carefully. He was watching the cabin, outside of which stood the pack mule and the horses. He stopped just where they judged he would, about twenty-five feet away from them. He put his right knee on the ground and they heard him cock his rifle. He rested his left elbow on the left knee and cuddled his cheek against the stock of the weapon, drawing a bead on the shack.

Wolf drew his Colt, and so did Dave. They had put their rifles on the ground beside them. From somewhere in the circle of armed men came a hail.

'Lobo, we have you surrounded. Come out with your hands up!'

Wolf nodded his head as a signal, and he and Dave stood up and moved silently forward. Their gaze was fastened on Jack, who knelt, sighting along the barrel of his Winchester. The two sixguns were pointed at his head. At the last moment he heard a slight noise behind him and turned. They saw astonishment, then sudden fear come into his eyes.

He cried hoarsely, 'No! No!' and tried to swing his rifle around. So rapidly did he make the motion that he lost his balance and fell on his side. He twisted his head and looked into the muzzles of the two Colts. He screamed.

Wolf got in the first shot. It was squarely between the man's eyes. Dave hesitated a second, even then reluctant to kill a defenseless man. When he finally did fire it was with the knowledge that he was pumping lead into a man already dead.

They picked up their rifles and hit for the horses.

CHAPTER SIXTEEN

They mounted the first two they came to, shoved their rifles into the boots and untied the other horses. They drove the horses before them, keeping them going by yelling and waving their arms. They did not hear the sounds behind them, shouts, curses, the crashing of underbrush as those who had encircled the cabin started the pursuit on foot.

They raced eastward, and when they reached

the end of the stretch of timber the fleeing horses began to fan out. There was no time to head them and keep them bunched; the two fugitives bore left and came to the trail which led to the Jupiter road. Once on this they made better time.

Wolf turned north on the Jupiter road, held to that course for a couple miles, then swung eastward and into terrain that was broken, where a trail must be followed slowly and painstakingly. He headed for a range of bare hills that rose ahead of them and entered the first defile they came to. Here, out of sight of the road, they pulled down to a walk.

'Got to save the horses,' said Wolf. 'They must be ready to go full out if we run into trouble.'

They rode for a while along the draw without speaking.

'Where are we heading for?'

'A place where we can hide our trail. We mustn't give them a hint where we're heading.'

They came to a flinty stretch and followed the ravine bed until it descended on a rocky flat. They crossed the flat, working eastward. They took to dry washes and gullies, climbing steadily into the hills. Twilight found them at the summit of the range and darkness gathered about them as they started the descent. It was completely dark when they reached the far side of the range and halted their horses to consider what next to do.

'Got any grub on your saddle?' Wolf asked.

'Not a bit. And no blanket roll. Not even a slicker. There's a canteen partly filled with water.'

'That means we don't eat. Let's find a place to camp.'

They turned southward and rode along the base of the hills looking for a spring or stream of some kind. They found none and made camp on a patch of grass where the horses could graze. They rested for an hour, smoking to kill their appetite, then started off again.

They rode until midnight, making the best time they could in the darkness, then halted, picketed the saddled horses and dropped to the ground.

'You sleep,' said Wolf. 'I'll watch.'

'All right. Wake me up in two hours.'

Wolf let him sleep four hours, then awakened him. The sky in the east was graying. 'You didn't wake me.'

'Reckon I fell asleep,' lied Wolf. 'Take a drink, tighten your belt and let's go.'

They rode on while the sky brightened. To their left was grazing land, and they saw cattle and, in the distance, the buildings of a ranch.

'Think we can get grub over there?' Dave asked.

'Can't risk it. Nobody must see us heading south. Pull in your belt another hole.'

They were following a serpentine course, traveling a greater distance than if they held to a straight line, but it was safer this way. Toward noon they came to a spring and stopped to let the horses drink and to refill their canteens.

'How far do you figure we've come?' Dave asked.

'We've ridden about forty miles. In a straight line, we're about twenty miles from where we started.'

'At that rate it'll take us another two days to reach the basin.'

'That's right.'

'And nothing to eat. Well, if you can stand it, so can I.'

'As long as the horses have grass and water we won't worry.'

They resumed their way as soon as the horses had eaten and rested. Wolf now stepped up the pace but still kept to the winding course which took them along the base of the hills. Dusk came and they halted again. Dave had not eaten since his cold lunch with Texas Jack at noon of the day before; Wolf had had nothing since supper on Friday. It was now Sunday evening.

They staked out the horses and once more dropped wearily to the ground.

'I'm beginning to see what you meant when you said this life wasn't all it's cracked up to be,' said Dave ruefully.

'You haven't seen the half of it. I've known

the time when I chewed the bark off a tree and relished green berries like they were apple pie.'

Wolf was feeling pretty good. Their chances of getting in the clear were about four to one in their favor, and it began to look as though Dave had been cured of his desire to become an outlaw. He had seen the seamy side of the life and he had not liked what he had seen. He had demonstrated his courage and fortitude to Wolf, and perhaps that was what he had really wanted to do. Perhaps now he would take one of Wolf's offers and settle down.

It rained that night, starting with a pelting downpour and then turning into a steady drizzle. They were soaked to the skin before they could ride into the hills and find shelter in a shallow cave. With the rain came a chill wind that bit right through their wet garments, and there was no dry wood for a fire. They huddled close together and shivered it out while the horses stood with drooping heads, rumps turned to the wind.

Wolf dozed; but Dave, as much as he wanted to, could not. He was much too miserable.

In the morning the rain stopped and the sun came out. They rode, sitting wet saddles and wearing wet clothing. They were so hungry that they were numb. The rangeland became poorer and the cattle and ranches fewer and farther apart. Noon came, and the last ranch they had passed was a dozen miles behind them.

Wolf took a look at Dave's pinched face and said, 'Reckon we'll eat.'

'Our saddles?' asked Dave bitterly.

'Beef. Before the cows disappear altogether. Take down your rope and we'll cut out one of those steers.' He pointed out over the rangeland where a few animals grazed.

Dave's face brightened and he hurriedly took down his rope. They rode towards the steers, who raced away at their approach.

'Wild as deer,' called Wolf. 'We'll have to do it the hard way. Take the brindle.'

They galloped after the brindle steer, which immediately went into full stride. He was a longhorn, all horn, hide and bone, but he could run like an antelope. They finally caught up with him, put their ropes on him and threw him. Wolf ran along his rope and cut the steer's throat.

They skinned down the hind quarters and detached them, cut off the feet and left them with the rest of the carcass for the buzzards, and rode back to their camp. They gathered wood and built a fire and roasted slices of the tough, stringy meat and started eating when it was still half raw, tearing at the flesh like wolves. They ate until they could hold no more, then roasted the rest of the meat and tied it to their saddles.

That night they camped at the foot of a spur of mountains which joined the range they had been following.

'These must be the hills that run back of our cabin,' said Wolf. 'Tomorrow will see us home, son.'

They ate more of their roasted steer meat and both slept the night through. They felt safe now...

★ ★ ★

Darkness overtook Sheriff Ed Grant before he came to the trail which led from the Jupiter road to the Acme mine. He knew he would not be able to find it in the dark, and in any event he was much too late to prevent whatever was to have happened that afternoon. He had intended riding to the mine and making inquiries, but he could not find the mine without first finding the trail, and that would have to wait until morning.

He had drawn rein and was debating the question when he heard a body of horsemen approaching the road from the east. He pulled back into a clump of trees and waited. The riders spoke loudly so that their voices carried over the thud of hoofs and he could distinguish the words.

'I don't believe they headed north,' said one. 'That El Lobo is foxy; he wants us to think he went east or north, so that means he went west or south.'

Ed saw their figures in the pale starlight and called to them. 'Sheriff Ed Grant talking, boys. You from the Acme mine?'

He rode out to meet them and flashed his star. The mine super introduced himself.

'I'm Harry Thompson and we're from the Acme. Never heard of a sheriff named Grant around here.'

'I'm out of my jurisdiction on a special assignment to get El Lobo. I heard you name him. What happened?'

Thompson told him the story from the time Texas Jack came to him with his proposition.

'There's something fishy about the deal,' Ed said, when the super had finished. 'You say El Lobo and Texas Jack worked together on the holdup. I happen to know they hate each other's guts. You're sure it was El Lobo?'

'That's what this Texas Jack told me, and that's what he called him down there in the ravine.'

'How long have you been following their trail?'

'Until the sun went down. We lost it then, and it wasn't light enough to pick it up again. We aim to bed down at Blakely's ranch a mile or so up the road, and tackle it again tomorrow.'

'I'll go with you to Blakely's and tomorrow I'll take you to Lobo's hide-out.'

They rode to Blakely's ranch and had supper.

After the meal, Ed took Harry Thompson aside and told him where the hide-out was located and how he had found it. He cautioned the super to say nothing to his men.

'Some of these boys should return to the mine. Do we need all of them?'

'No. You, me and three others should be enough.'

The next morning they purchased supplies from Blakely, and the five of them headed south. It was six in the evening when they sighted Santa Anita.

'We won't go through the town,' decided Ed. 'Lobo may have friends there who might tip him off. We'll circle to the hills behind the cabin and get to him that way.'

They turned off into the hills, camped for one night, and on Sunday worked to a point behind the cabin. They found a grassy hollow where they could picket the horses, and a nest of rocks which overlooked the basin where they could camp. They settled down to wait. All day Monday they waited, but Wolf and his partner did not arrive.

It was dusk on Tuesday evening when the man who was guarding the horses came running into the rock cluster. 'They're coming! I saw them across a rise not half a mile from where we staked out the horses. They're heading along that trail that runs through the clearing where they cut the trees.'

Ed outlined their strategy. 'It's getting dark. Let them go to the cabin. They'll be dog tired and they think they're safe. They'll eat, turn in and sleep like logs. Along toward morning, we'll slip down there on foot and surround the cabin. We'll have them dead to rights and none of us will get hurt.'

It was a sensible plan. El Lobo had reached the end of the trail...

CHAPTER SEVENTEEN

The basin looked to Dave like the land of milk and honey, the little cabin, a palace. The weight of fear and hardship fell from him and his tired body straightened.

'We're home, Dad,' he said.

Wolf nearly fell off his horse. 'What's that you called me?'

'Dad. Guess it just slipped out.'

'Let it slip out again. I like it.'

'I guess I've been thinking of you as dad for some time. Just seems to fit somehow. And your calling me son—'

'I know. Reckon if I had one I'd want him to be a lot like you.'

Dave waved a hand towards the basin. 'Never looked so good to me before. When we finish the house I think I'll ask Downing for a job as cowhand.' He added quickly, 'That is, unless you want me—'

'To go along with me? No, I've pulled my last job. I want to sit down in that old rawhide chair and just look on. I've got a powerful lot of resting to do. I'm tired, son; tired.'

The sun had gone and the soft afterglow was in the sky. They rode down the trail to the corral, stripped their horses and turned them in. Wolf got grain for them and Dave forked hay over the rails. They carried their rigs to the wagon shed and dropped them into the back of the buckboard. They went into the house carrying what was left of the meat. A flour sack was draped over something on the table; Wolf removed it and they saw two loaves of freshly baked bread and a dried apple pie.

'Pat's been here,' said Wolf.

Dave tore a big chunk off one of the loaves and started eating ravenously. Wolf did the same.

'Reckon there's no danger of spoiling our appetites,' he said. 'I'll cook up a stew of beef, potatoes, and onions. How does that sound?'

'Great!'

Wolf built a fire in the stove and Dave went outside to the spring and fetched a pail of fresh water. Wolf peeled potatoes and onions, cut up some of the partially roasted meat and put everything into a pot of water which he set on the front of the stove. They talked while the meal cooked and Dave told Wolf in detail about his meeting the man who called himself Tom Smith and the outcome of that meeting.

It was a wonderful meal and they ate like half-starved animals. When they could hold no more, Dave pushed back his chair and stretched his legs beneath the table.

'Tomorrow evening I'll ride over to the ranch and thank Pat for the bread and pie. I've treated her right mean. And I'll tell Downing I'll take that job just as soon as we finish the house.'

They washed up the dishes and Wolf went outside while the daylight lingered to scan the surroundings through the binoculars. He came in, satisfied.

'Everything peaceful. They can't follow us here, son.'

Dave was already shedding his clothes. Wolf began to undress. 'Have to get rid of those horses first thing in the morning...'

They rolled in their blankets while it was still dusk and fell asleep almost at once. When Wolf awoke, the windows were gray with dawn and Dave was still asleep in his bunk.

Wolf got up and dressed. It was still too dark to see much with the glasses, so he kindled a fire in the stove, put the coffee pot on, and filled the kettle from the bucket. Dave heard him working and awakened. He kicked off the covers, stretched, sprang out of bed.

He pulled on his clothes, went over to the

wash bench and filled the basin with cold water. He splashed and snorted, dried on a flour sack towel, went to the back door and opened it to throw out the water.

He leaped back and slammed the door, dropping the basin. Wolf was at the table slicing bacon and looked up quickly. Dave picked up the bar and thrust it into its sockets, then wheeled.

'There's somebody out there!' he whispered tensely. 'Hiding in the wagon shed. He pulled back out of sight, but I saw him!'

Wolf glided to the chair beside his bunk and picked up his sixgun. There was a front door and a back door and a window in each of the two side walls. He ran to the one facing the west. It was too gloomy in the cabin for anybody outside to see him, but he could see them.

By looking at an angle toward the north, he could see part of the shed, and just inside it crouched a man. He held a rifle with its butt under his arm, ready to snap it up into firing position. From where he was he could command that window and the back door.

Directly opposite the window was the rear corner of the house they were building. It was about a hundred and fifty feet distant, and extended beyond the front of the cabin. Five tiers of logs had been erected, and behind them, directly across from the window, he saw the hatted head of a man. Behind the logs at the front of the building was a third. These two had the west window covered, and the one in front could also command the front door.

'They're—out there?' Dave's mouth had suddenly gone dry.

'Yes.'

Wolf crossed the room to the other window. Looking at an angle toward the rear of the cabin he could see the big woodpile and knew there would be a man hiding behind it. Some fifty feet from the cabin and running parallel with it was the gully through which the spring overflow ran. Above its near bank he could see the head of still another man. He could cover both the east window and the front door from where he was stationed. They were trapped.

For a moment all the strength drained out of Wolf, and for the first time he was uncertain what to do. Alone, he would have made a break while the light was still uncertain, bolting through the rear door like a rocket, trying to get the man in the shed and then the one behind the woodpile. If luck was with him, he might manage to get one of the horses before the others could reach him. Had he been alone he would have tried this; but Dave was with him.

'How many are there?' asked Dave.

'I saw four. I think there's another behind the woodpile. Oh, why did it have to happen now!'

‘We’ll shoot our way out!’

‘They’d mow us down.’ He seized Dave by the shoulders, gripped him hard. ‘Listen, son! Take the bucket and go out there like you’re going for water. Leave your gun behind. When they jump you, throw up your hands. They haven’t got a thing on you; they think it was me in the holdup with Texas Jack.’

Dave gazed steadily at him. ‘And what about you?’

‘Forget about me! Do as I say.’

‘And leave you here to die like a rat? No! We go out together, or we don’t go out at all.’

Wolf shook him angrily. ‘For God’s sake do as I tell you! I’m done, no matter how you look at it. If they don’t kill me now they’ll hang me later. Give yourself up, and while they’re busy with you I’ll try to break out.’

Dave considered this briefly, brushed it aside. ‘It won’t work, and you know it won’t. They know I’ve seen them and they know you’re in here with me. I stay with you.’

Wolf took his hands from the boy’s shoulders. ‘I’m not going to see you killed for a few pounds of painted lead! Stay here and you’ll have to fight. In the fight you’ll kill somebody. It will be too late then to save you. For God’s sake, do what I tell you!’

Dave shook his head. ‘I got you into this; I’ll stick with you, no matter how it ends.’

Wolf knew that no argument would move

him. He had plenty of his old man's stubbornness in him. Wolf sat down on the bunk and put his head in his hands, thinking, scheming.

Through the silence came a voice: 'Wolf, this is Ed Grant. We got you pinned down. Your one chance is to come out with your hands in the air.'

Wolf raised his head, called, 'I swore you'd never take me alive, Ed. That still goes.'

'Then you'd better come out shooting!'

'There's a young feller in here with me. He had nothing to do with the Acme holdup. It was just Texas Jack and me.'

'That's a lie!' shouted Dave angrily.

'Let him come out if he's in the clear.'

Wolf sprang up, seized Dave by an arm. 'There's your chance, Dave! He can't prove a thing against you! Get out now while you can. Please, son!'

Dave set his lips, shook his head. 'I got you into this, Wolf, and I'm not leaving. That's flat and final.'

Wolf shook his head in frustration and went back and sat down on the bunk. Dave followed him.

'If we can stall them until dark,' he said, 'we'll have a better chance of making it.'

'They'll build fires in front and in back so they can watch both doors. The windows don't open; we'd have to break them and that would warn them. The only—'

He broke off, his gaze going to the floor.

The planks were nailed to beams which ran lengthwise from the lowest tier of logs. He got up, got the poker from the stove, wedged the crooked end of it between two planks and started prying. Dave, getting the idea, crouched down and put his fingers under the end of the plank as Wolf raised it. They pulled the plank away, put it to one side.

The heavy stringers were three in number, one running down the middle of the cabin from one end to the other, the others spaced evenly between this and the side walls. There was a space about six inches deep between floor boards and ground.

Excitement gripped Dave. 'We can dig under the wall! They'll be watching the doors and the windows. When it's dark we worm out under the bottom log!'

'Maybe. Maybe, son. We'll need a lot of luck, but it's about the only way left to us. We'd have to snake our way to the gully on our bellies, an inch at a time. If we can make that gully, we'll have a fifty-fifty chance.'

'Then let's start digging.'

'All our tools are in the shed. Only thing we have to dig with is the stove shovel.'

Dave ran to the stove and came back with the small shovel used in removing ashes. He got down on his stomach and started digging out the four-foot space between the stringer and the east wall. He put the dirt he removed into the space on the other side of the stringer. Wolf moved about watching the windows, although he was pretty sure they would not try rushing the cabin. After a while, Wolf dug while Dave watched.

Ed Grant hailed them again. 'Better come out, Wolf. We got grub and water and can hold out longer than you can.'

Wolf did not answer him.

When noon came, they had enlarged the space beneath the flooring to a depth of eighteen inches and had dug halfway under the bottom log. They must wait until dark before finishing. Hope soared high and they were quietly jubilant. A little more digging and they would be able to squeeze beneath the lower log.

They ate their long-delayed breakfast and discussed plans. Once they were outside the cabin, no attempt would be made to get their horses from the corral. They would snake down to the gully and into it, work their way to the spring, and follow the base of the hill until it was safe to head across the basin to the ranch. It would take them all of two hours to cross, but once there they could get horses.

They spent the afternoon watching and waiting. Wolf made up two packages of food to take along. The sky was overcast, making it gloomy in the cabin, and they knew they were safe from sniping shots if they kept away from the windows. Ed Grant seemed satisfied to wait it out, and the two men inside pulled the table to the front end of the cabin and sat down to a game of cassino.

At three o'clock in the afternoon Ed Grant tried once more. 'Hello in the cabin! We're not waiting much longer. Better come out while you have the chance.'

This time Wolf answered: 'Reckon you'll have to come in and persuade us, Ed.'

'Do you think they'll rush us?' asked Dave.

'Not likely in the daytime, but you never can tell. If they do, I don't want you to be in it. Throw away your gun and shove your hands up. There's no sense in your throwing away your life just to show me how brave you are. You've already done that, son.'

'Quit talking about my giving up. If they rush us, we can stop them cold. All we got to do is hold them off until after dark and we'll both be in the clear.'

Wolf had his silent doubts about this. Dave had a lot to learn about Ed Grant.

A few minutes later they heard men moving stealthily about in the rear of the cabin. They put aside their cards and took up their sixguns.

'They're mighty brave back there,' said Dave scornfully. 'There are no windows we can shoot through.'

Wolf felt apprehension. There must be some

reason for their moving about, and he thought he knew what it was. He was sure a little later when the sound of a soft crackling reached them. Then a little curl of smoke seeped under the back door.

'They're firing the cabin!' cried Dave. 'Wolf, they're going to burn us out!'

'Yes,' said Wolf grimly. 'It'll take time, but the logs are dry, and once the smoke fills the place, we're licked. We go out and get shot, or we stay in and burn.'

'The dirty cowards! Wolf, let's rush them!'

'That's what they're expecting us to do.'

'But we can't just squat down here and roast!'

He jumped in the hole they had dug, snatched up the shovel. Wolf pulled him out.

'You'd have less chance that way than through the door. There are two men watching this side of the house; they'll see the dirt flying long before the hole's big enough to crawl through. If I've got to go, it will be on my feet with a gun in my hand.'

The flames were crackling loudly now, and the smoke was coming in all around the door.

'Let's charge them now,' said Dave tightly. His face was hard and strained, but there was no fear in his eyes. He picked up his rifle.

'Leave the rifle,' said Wolf. 'It'll just be in your way. Close work calls for short guns. Wait a minute.'

He went to his bunk, got a sock. He carried it

to the pile of dirt between the stringers and started filling it. Dave watched.

'What's that for?'

'Close work. More of a punch in it than a bare fist.'

'A gun barrel suits me better. You ready?'

They walked to the front door.

Wolf said, 'You take down the bar, and when I give the word, yank the door open wide. I'll go out first; you follow me close.'

'I'll go first,' said Dave firmly. 'I'm tired of you protecting me.'

They looked hard at each other. Wolf did not protest. He thrust out a hand. 'Good luck, son.'

Dave gripped the hand. 'Good luck yourself, Dad.'

'Take down the bar,' said Wolf quietly.

Dave turned and lifted the bar. Wolf was close behind him. He directed his gaze at the exact spot behind Dave's right ear that he wanted to strike, raised the filled sock and brought it down with all his force.

Dave's knees buckled and he folded up like an empty sack.

CHAPTER EIGHTEEN

Wolf bent over him, saw that he was breathing. He lifted him by the shoulders and dragged him to one side. He took a deep breath, wrenched open the door and went through it as though hurled from a catapult.

The man behind the wall of the new house was about the same distance from him as was Ed. He had a glimpse of Ed scrambling up the gully bank and flashed a look at the other. The man was swinging the rifle in an arc to lead his target, and Wolf snapped two quick shots at him.

He did not know which of them hit, but the man went down behind the logs. Wolf had to get into that gully to stand any chance whatever, so he veered to his left and raced towards Ed Grant. There was nothing cowardly about Ed; he had wanted a face-to-face meeting with El Lobo and now he had it. He scrambled over the bank and came running to meet Wolf.

Wolf passed beyond the front corner of the cabin and was now exposed to the fire of the man behind the woodpile. He heard the rifle crack and at the same moment felt a numbing smash on his left shoulder which nearly knocked him off his feet. His left arm dropped limp, the shoulder joint shattered. He was thirty feet from Ed. He felt no pain, but the shock and the physical reaction blurred his vision, and the figure before him seemed to undulate like movement in a warped mirror.

He fired in desperation and must have missed, for the figure kept up its gyrations. He did not realize it, but he was running in a weaving, staggering course keeping his feet only by sheer force of will and that stubbornness which would not let him quit. He fired again. Dimly he could hear Ed shouting, 'Drop it, George! Drop the gun!'

There was another stumbling impact against his side and Wolf staggered to the right. He fired again, then red flame exploded directly in front of him and the heavy slug knocked him off his feet and he hit the ground hard. His sight was blurred and a furnace was roaring in his head, but he raised the Colt and fired it. There was no explosion, just a series of clicks as the hammer fell on empty shells. He heard Ed yell, 'Quit it, George! Damn it, don't you know when you're licked?'

Who was he calling George? Oh, yes; that was his name. George Singleton. Mary's husband. Dave's father. For the first time since he had taken to outlawry, his one-time friend had called him by his proper name.

The raised arm fell, the wild eyes closed. He was numb and tired and it was very dark.

Ed took the gun from lax fingers and shoved it in his belt. On his face was written relief, admiration, and a deep pity. El Lobo was finished; that accounted for the relief. The admiration was for a man who knew no fear, who still fought on with a smashed shoulder, a slug through his stomach, and another one in his chest. The pity was for a man whom he had called friend and whom the law had made it his duty to capture or kill.

He stood looking down at George Singleton with these things in his face until he remembered that the job was not yet finished. The man from the woodpile was coming along the side of the cabin.

'Get back!' Ed called. 'There's another one inside. Tell the others to keep their posts.'

The man hurried back to the woodpile, calling to his mate in the wagon shed.

The man behind the wall of logs called, 'He got Jake, Ed. Creased him, looks like.'

'Then leave him and watch that side.'

Ed ran to his right, his gun ready, watching both the front entrance, now wide open, and the side window. He reached the corner of the cabin, and yelled, 'Come out, you! Leave your gun and keep your hands high.'

There was no answer.

Ed edged along the windowless front to the door, poked his gun ahead of him and looked slantingly through the entrance. He saw the figure of a young man lying face-down on the floor. He put his gun on the figure, moved forward. A quick glance showed him nobody else inside the cabin. He stepped over the sill and picked up the gun which lay beside the boy's hand.

He saw a man's sock stuffed with something.

He picked it up and found the stuffing to consist of dirt and gravel. He stood there looking at it, frowning perplexedly, then knelt and turned the boy over on his back.

He was unconscious, but breathing, and there was no sign of an open wound. He crouched there for some seconds gazing at the face with its closed eyes, and suddenly he saw a resemblance to one he had known more than twenty years before.

He opened the boy's collar to look for a wound and saw the string with the locket at its end. He opened the locket and sat staring at the gentle features of a young girl, the girl who had married George Singleton.

He knew then.

He closed the locket and replaced it. The boy's hat had fallen off and he felt behind both ears. There was a swelling behind the right one. He shook his head, got to his feet and mechanically brushed off his knees. George Singleton had done this to his son to save him. The question was, did the boy know El Lobo was his father?

He had laid the sock to one side; now he emptied it and let it fall. He stepped outside, called to the man over at the house.

'You can take care of Jake now. And tell the others it's over.'

They came around to the front of the building. They looked down at the unconscious boy, then at Ed.

'How'd you get him, Ed?' asked one. 'I didn't hear any shooting.'

'He was slugged,' said Ed briefly. 'Help me carry him outside, then get buckets of water and put out that fire.'

They carried Dave out of the cabin and laid him on the grass, then left to fight the fire. Ed crossed to where George Singleton lay, knelt down, put his ear to El Lobo's chest. There was a very faint heartbeat.

Motion out on the range caught his attention, and he saw a body of riders coming at a sweeping gallop. They would be from the Downing ranch. No, not the Downing ranch, George Singleton's ranch.

He went into the cabin and came out with a straw mattress from a bunk. He laid it beside El Lobo, raised him carefully and laid him on it. He covered him with a blanket, then went to the stream and wet his scarf. He came back and wiped Wolf's face, folded the wet scarf and put it on his forehead. Then he squatted on his heels and looked somberly into the grim face of the man he had hunted for twenty years.

In his mind he reviewed the events just before and after he had met George. He remembered when George and Mary were married, he remembered when George had left his young wife to join Quantrill, he remembered George's return, and the hard luck which seemed to pursue him.

He remembered the holdup and the killing of the marshal that had put him on George's trail. He had spent twenty years on that trail, but now that he had reached its end there was no exultation in him. He shook his head. He had been forty when he started out, now he was sixty, and mighty tired.

Mary . . . He remembered when she had sold out and gone back to her folks in Wyoming. She had pledged him then to keep El Lobo's real name out of print. She must have known then that the boy was on his way. He had received one letter from her after she reached Wyoming. She had borne George a son, but he must never know it; and she begged Ed never to let word of his father reach the boy. Well, he had kept that pledge.

George could not have known that he had a son on the night he had met the boy in that saloon, but something had impelled the Lone Wolf to defend the boy, to aid him to escape. Eventually he must have learned that the boy was his son; the question remained, did the boy know El Lobo was his father.

'Ed.'

The voice was faint but distinct, and Ed glanced quickly down. George Singleton's eyes were open and they were clear. Ed bent over.

'Yes, George?'

'Davey—he's inside.'

'We fetched him out. He'll be all right.'

'Thank God! He wanted—to stay—with me. You know—?'

'Yes, George. He's your boy. Yours and Mary's.'

Misery filled the eyes. 'She never told me!'

'Did you tell him?'

'No. Ed you—mustn't!'

'I'll see to it that he never knows, George.'

'Be good to him. He wasn't—in the—deal. It was me and Texas Jack.'

The eyes closed wearily, then snapped open again. 'Promise me, Ed! Give him—chance! For Mary's sake.'

He was panting weakly. Ed reached down, took a hand, pressed it. 'For Mary's sake,' Sheriff Ed Grant said softly.

The dying man's eyes closed again. He gave a little sigh, went limp. Ed sighed heavily and got up. There was nothing more he could do for George Singleton except to forget that he had ever had another name than El Lobo.

The riders were quite close now, and coming fast.

He looked at Dave and saw him stir. He pushed himself slowly to an elbow, then got dazedly to his feet, then came slowly and uncertainly towards Ed. He came to where El Lobo lay and dropped to his knees. He put his head against Wolf's chest, then straightened slowly.

'He's dead. And it's all my fault! He knocked me out to keep me from going with him. He never would let me go with him, not even at the end.'

He turned suddenly, threw himself face down on the ground and buried his head in his arms. Ed saw his shoulders heave. Ed cleared his throat and looked about him. The fire was nearly out. The riders were racing for the back of the cabin except for one of them, the girl he remembered as Pat Downing. He looked back at Dave, who was now gazing into the face of the dead outlaw.

'He was a good man,' said Dave huskily. 'The best I ever knew. He treated me like I was his son.'

'You knew who he was?'

'Yes. Wolf, or El Lobo. Here in the basin he was Christopher Jones.'

'That wasn't his right name; you know that?'

'I guessed that it wasn't, but he never told me what his real was. Do you know?'

'Nobody knows. I reckon nobody ever will.'

Pat rode up, dropped quickly from her horse, ran to fall on her knees beside Dave. She cried, 'Uncle Chris! Davey, he's—dead?'

'Yes.'

Ed said, 'You didn't know who he was, Miss Downing?'

'Of course I did. He was Christopher Jones. I told you that.'

'He was the man known as El Lobo.'

'Oh no! You must be mistaken!'

'No'm. I've been hunting him off and on for twenty years.'

She turned to Dave, her face troubled. 'Davey, did *you* know?'

'I knew, Pat. I—'

Grant cut in sharply: 'He knew, but El Lobo had befriended him and he wouldn't tell. He never helped El Lobo on a job. Did you, son?'

'No. No, but I—'

Again Ed cut him short. 'That's what he told me before he died. He gave me the whole story. Him and Texas Jack held up the mine shipment. It was a put-up job by Texas Jack and the Acme people to get him caught or killed. The boy here heard about it and rode after El Lobo to try to stop him. He was too late and tagged along with El Lobo. We traced them here. That's the confession of a dying man. He gave you a clean bill, son, and as far as I'm concerned that ends it.'

Dave started to protest, saw the warning look in the sheriff's eyes, heard Pat's fervent, 'Thank God!' and felt the convulsive pressure of the arm she had put about him. Wolf had wanted it that way; everything the man had done for him had been for his good. Confessing his guilt would not bring Wolf back.

'So,' said Ed, 'you're completely in the clear.' He strode away, calling, 'How you boys making out back there?'

They knelt side by side, and now Dave's arms circled Pat's waist.

'He was good,' said Pat. 'I don't care what they say, he was good.' She started to cry, and Dave drew her to him, stroking her hair.

'He was the only father I ever knew. I think he loved me. I know I loved him. He wanted me to take a job on the ranch. Pat, I reckon it will be yours and your grandfather's now. There's nobody else.'

She looked up at him, tears on her cheeks.

'There is somebody else, Davey. That Sunday when you came over to dinner and we went for a ride, Uncle Chris wrote out a will. My grandfather and two of the hands witnessed it. Uncle Chris left the ranch and everything on it to you.'

'He didn't!'

'Yes. I guess you were just about the only one he really loved. He told me he had no wife, no family. Davey, I'm so glad for you!'

'I can't believe it. We only knew each other for a couple weeks.'

'It's like I said. He loved you. Sometimes I thought he liked me, but he loved you.'

'And he left me the ranch and everything on it!' He looked down at her. 'Everything on it; you know what that means, Pat?'

She nodded gravely. 'Yes, Davey, I think I do.'

He kissed her on the lips. Then, very solemnly, very reverently, he bent over and kissed El Lobo on the forehead.

'Good-by, Dad,' he whispered. 'And thanks; thank you so much.'